ARE YOU SURE
YOU WANT TO KNOW?

SCENE OF THE CRIME

As rain peppered the roof, Nikki made her way to the loft and from that position high over the living area, she took another picture, of the blackened fireplace below, with its rock face and thick mantel. How had Blondell and her kids ended up here?

She'd seen all she needed to have seen and what little light was left, filtering through the windows, was swiftly fading. The place felt haunted, as if whatever evil had gone down that night had seeped into the walls and floorboards of the old building, as if a residue of the depravity still lingered.

From the loft, she took a step onto the stairs.

Thud!

She nearly tripped at the sound, then caught herself by grabbing the rail.

She was alone.

Right?

No one else was here and no one had followed her. She'd checked.

Her instincts on alert, Nikki's nerves were strung tight as she started downward again and tried to ignore the fact that she felt as if she were being observed, her every move noted . . .

Books by Lisa Jackson

Stand-Alones

SEE HOW SHE DIES
FINAL SCREAM
RUNNING SCARED
WHISPERS
TWICE KISSED
UNSPOKEN
DEEP FREEZE
FATAL BURN
MOST LIKELY TO DIE
WICKED GAME
WICKED LIES
SOMETHING WICKED
WICKED WAYS
SINISTER
WITHOUT MERCY
YOU DON'T WANT TO
    KNOW
CLOSE TO HOME

**Anthony Paterno/Cahill
    Family Novels**

IF SHE ONLY KNEW
ALMOST DEAD

**Rick Bentz/Reuben
    Montoya Novels**

HOT BLOODED
COLD BLOODED
SHIVER
ABSOLUTE FEAR
LOST SOULS
MALICE
DEVIOUS

**Pierce Reed/Nikki Gillette
    Novels**

THE NIGHT BEFORE
THE MORNING AFTER
TELL ME

**Selena Alvarez/Regan
    Pescoli Novels**

LEFT TO DIE
CHOSEN TO DIE
BORN TO DIE
AFRAID TO DIE
READY TO DIE
DESERVES TO DIE

Published by Kensington Publishing Corporation

LISA JACKSON

TELL ME

ZEBRA BOOKS
KENSINGTON PUBLISHING CORP.
http://www.kensingtonbooks.com

ZEBRA BOOKS are published by

Kensington Publishing Corp.
119 West 40th Street
New York, NY 10018

All Kensington titles, imprints, and distributed lines are available at special quantity discounts for bulk purchases for sales promotion, premiums, fund-raising, educational, or institutional use.

Special book excerpts or customized printings can also be created to fit specific needs. For details, write or phone the office of the Kensington Special Sales Manager: Attn. Special Sales Department. Kensington Publishing Corp., 119 West 40th Street, New York, NY 10018. Phone: 1-800-221-2647.

Zebra and the Z logo Reg. U.S. Pat. & TM Off.

First Kensington Books Hardcover/Trade Printing: July 2013
First Zebra Books Mass-Market Paperback Printing: March 2014
ISBN-13: 978-1-4201-1854-4
ISBN-10: 1-4201-1854-4

First Zebra Books Electronic Edition: March 2014
eISBN-13: 978-1-4201-3410-0
eISBN-10: 1-4201-3410-8

10 9 8 7

Printed in the United States of America

Dedicated to the people of Savannah.
I love your fair city, even if I do take liberties with it.

Prologue

His hand was cool as it slid up her leg, smoothly brushing her calf, tickling and teasing, causing her spine to tingle and a warmth to start in the deepest part of her. Ever upward it traveled, slipping effortlessly against her, nearly undulating.

"Don't," she wanted to say but couldn't, because her voice wouldn't work, and really, she didn't want him to stop. His touch was magical. Divine. And downright dangerous. She knew all this even though she hadn't yet woken.

Hovering somewhere between consciousness and sleep, she thought she was on the edge of a dream, a warm sensation that lulled her into wanting to snuggle deeper inside the covers.

Still, his touch was sensual. Arousing. And because of it, she was in trouble. Big trouble. But she couldn't stop. Even now, when she knew it was the worst time ever for him to be sliding his hand along her bare skin.

The smell of wood smoke filled her nostrils, and the bed was warm and cozy, even though she heard the sigh of the wind as it rattled the windows.

Amity vaguely remembered that she wasn't at home, that her mother, ogre that she was, had forced her and her two younger siblings out here in the middle of no-damned-where for the night.

That's right. Amity wasn't in her room at the house her mother rented. There was no lock on the door, no way to ensure privacy.

But Mother was out or asleep, and now Amity was with him.

Right?

Did that make sense?

On the edge of dreamland, she decided he'd taken a risk to come to her . . . of course he had. Despite the danger. But she'd dozed and now was still in that blissful state between being fully awake and dreamland. Somehow avoiding Blondell's watchful eye, he must've sneaked into the cabin and slid beneath the covers. God, he was good. Experienced. Made her feel like a woman, not a girl.

Of course, not everything was perfect, and now . . . now there was big trouble. Amity had needed to talk to someone about it, so she'd called her friend. She'd begged Nikki to sneak out and come to the house by the lake, and her friend had promised she would, but like everyone else in Amity's pathetic life, Nikki had abandoned her. Well, good. Then she wouldn't have to share her secret.

For now.

And *he* had slipped in unnoticed, come to her, loved her. For the first time in her life, she felt secure.

Yet something wasn't right. Even in her semi-dreamlike state, she knew they had to be careful.

Quiet.

Nearly silent.

Hoping the darkness was enough of a cover, though soon, of course, they would let the world know of their love. That thought warmed her as much as his touch.

Her lips were dry, her mind still fuzzy with sleep. She thought she heard a dog barking in the distance but wasn't sure, and it didn't matter, of course. Nothing did but him. Realizing that since he'd started touching her, he hadn't uttered a word, she said softly, "Come closer." Anticipating his weight, anxious to feel his body against hers, she was disappointed. All she knew was his arm, long and fluid, sliding across her bare skin.

Was he just being careful?

Or was it something more?

It was strange that he wasn't pressing himself urgently against her, wasn't nuzzling her neck, or reaching around her to touch her breast. He should be tangling his hands in her hair, his lips hot and anxious as they found her own.

But tonight he was aloof. Playing his game. Toying with her.

And Mother was so close. Wasn't she? Or had Blondell left, assuming yet again that Amity would babysit the younger ones? These days, who knew?

However, him being here was dangerous. They couldn't be caught together. Not yet. She writhed a little, anxious for more of his touch, but he kept stroking her, sliding his arm against her.

With his silky smooth touch, he trailed his hand along her thighs, along the outside of her hips, and ever upward, across her rib cage, trailing the length of her.

Oh, Lord, this was magical. And playing with fire. Which, of course, she already had. That's why she was in so much trouble already.

His arm slid between her breasts and ever upward, yet somehow managed to move against the skin all along her thigh and abdomen and . . . ? Wait! That wasn't right.

She was waking now, dreamland fading . . .

Letting out her breath in a sigh, she opened a bleary eye. The room was dark, aside from the merest light from the fire and the lowest setting of the kerosene lantern on a nearby table. Lying on the hide-a-bed tucked beneath the loft of the cabin, she heard rain beating against the roof. A hard, steady tattoo. But . . . she was alone. There was no one with her. He wasn't stretched out on the mattress beside her. No. It was all a dream.

The only others in the old shack were her brother and sister.

Just Blythe and Niall, upstairs in the loft, sleeping. And Mom was probably still on the porch. That's where she said she was going when you started dropping off, when she grabbed her opened bottle of wine and a glass and walked through the connecting door.

Still, something seemed off. The dream was so real. But if *he* wasn't here, beside her, then what the devil . . . ?

Alarm bells clanged through her mind.

Someone, no, make that some*thing* had been touching her and even now . . . Oh, Mother Mary! . . . it was rubbing up against her, only to stop suddenly, the length of it trailing over her.

Oh, *no!*

Hissss!

The sibilant sound echoed through her brain.

For the love of Jesus! No!

Screaming in sheer terror, she frantically threw back the covers and scrambled backward on the bed in a single motion. The snake, its reptilian eyes reflecting the red of the dying embers, hoisted back its sharp, triangular head.

Shrieking, trying to fly off the bed, her legs tangling in the covers. "Mom!"

Too late!

Quick as lightning, the snake struck, its coppery head still visible. Fangs sunk into her leg, hot pain searing.

"Mom!" Amity screamed, reaching for the side table, her fingers touching the base of the kerosene lamp, turned so low as to barely glow as the snake slithered quickly off the bed. "Oh, God, oh, God, oh, God! Mom!" In a full-blown panic, Amity grabbed the lamp and threw it hard against the wall, glass shattering, kerosene bursting in a blinding flash that quickly died.

The snake.

Where the hell was the snake?

I'm going to die . . . Oh dear God. "Mom! Where the hell are you?

"Mom! Help! Snake!" she yelled. Afraid to get off the damned bed, she turned toward the door to the porch, only to see a dark figure hiding in the shadows. "Help! Oh, God, I've been . . ." Her heart was pounding, sweat collecting on her body. "Mom?" she whispered, scared out of her mind. "The snake just bit me! It's still in the house, oh, holy crap! Did you hear me?" Tears began running down her face, her heart pounding wildly. "We have to get to the hospital!"

Movement.

Was the figure one person? Or two?

In the dark, without her contacts, Amity couldn't tell. Didn't care. Were they kissing? For the love of God! No, maybe wrestling?

"Mom!" No, wait. That wasn't Mom, was it? It was only one person, kind of wobbly on their feet. Or not? Chaotic footsteps pounded in the loft above her. Her siblings!

"Niall! Blythe! Stay upstairs!" she cried when she saw, in the faint light, silhouetted in the figure's hand, the image of a pistol.

Was Mom going to shoot the snake? In here? In the dark? Why the hell didn't she turn on the lights and—

She realized the gun's muzzle was aimed at her.

"No!" Cowering in the corner of the sofa bed, she pointed toward the corner where the snake had slithered. "It's over there. A damned copperhead, I think. Mom—"

Blam!

A deafening blast roared through the cabin.

A flash of light.

The muzzle of a gun as it kicked back a little.

Amity's body slammed against the musty pillows of the couch, pain searing through her abdomen.

Disbelief tore through her mind. She'd been shot? Someone had shot her? No way . . . but the blood running through her fingers told a different story, confirmed to her unwilling mind that someone wanted her dead.

She was still screaming as the world went black.

December 2nd
First Interview

" **J**ust tell me what you know about that night. Let me tell your side of the story to the rest of the world. If you didn't try to kill the children, if you didn't mean to hurt them, then tell me the truth. Let me be your mouthpiece. Trust me, I can help!"

The eyes beyond the glass don't so much as blink. I'm not sure she's even heard my question. Then again, did someone who'd tried to murder children in cold blood ever hear anyone else? Ever really try to explain?

As I sit in my tiny stall, an open booth with an uncomfortable stool, a heavy telephone receiver and thick prison glass separating the free from the incarcerated, I try my best to be convincing and earnest, hoping to wring the truth from the person on the other side of the clear barrier.

But it seems impossible.

The prisoner suspects I'm up to something. That I'm using the information I might get from this interview for my own purposes, which, of course, isn't far from the truth.

As I stare through the smudged glass at the woman who's agreed to be contacted, a woman whom the public has reviled, someone with whom I've been through so much, I wonder if I'll ever get through, if the truth will ever be told. Suspicion smolders in her eyes, and something more too, something almost hidden. Hopelessness? Fear? Or is it accusation?

As if she knows.

But then, why wouldn't she?

It isn't as if we're strangers.

My heart trips a bit, and I want to bolt, to hide. But I force myself to sit on the worn-down stool where thousands have sat before me.

"I can help," I plead, and cringe at the tone of desperation in my own voice.

Her expression falters a bit, and even dressed in drab prison garb, without makeup, her once-shiny hair streaked with gray, a few pesky wrinkles appearing on what was once flawless skin, she's a beauty, with high cheekbones, large eyes, and full lips. The years since the horrific crime of which she's accused have been surprisingly kind.

There is noise in the hallway, on my side of the thick window, whispered voices from other booths filtering my way. There is no privacy here, not with the cameras mounted on the ceiling and the guards watching over the line of free people attempting to speak to inmates.

I hear sobbing from the elderly woman to my right as she tries to speak in low tones. She shuffled in before me and wears a bandanna on her head, dabbing at her eyes with a hanky. Her wedding ring is loose on her finger, her sadness palpable.

The stool to my left is vacant. A man in his thirties with tattoos climbing up his arms and a neatly trimmed soul patch, the only hair on his head, storms out angrily, his footsteps pounding away, echoing the loneliness of the worn souls who reside within.

But I can't be distracted by the hum of conversation, nor the shuffle of footsteps, nor the occasional burst of bitter laughter. There is little time, and I want only one small thing: the truth and all of it.

"Come on, I can help. Really," I insist, but in my little nook, where I can sense the prison cameras filming this interview, there is only silence as she`stares through the glass at me, quiet as death.

Chapter 1

"I know, I know. I'm working on it. Really! I just need a little more time to come up with the right story!" Nikki Gillette glanced up at the skylight as rain drizzled down the pane. Above the glass, the sky was a gloomy shade of gray, the clouds thick with a coming twilight hurrying across the city. Beneath the window, inside her loft and curled into a ball on the top of the daybed, lay her cat, Jennings, his eyes closed, his golden tail twitching slightly as he slept. Seeing him, Nikki reminded herself yet again that she needed to pick up Mikado at the groomer's tomorrow. Her head was so full of her own problems, she'd forgotten him today. Luckily, Ruby had assured her she could pick up the dog tomorrow at no extra fee, a kindness she wasn't generally known for.

Hunched over her desk, Nikki held the phone to her ear with one hand and fiddled with a pen in the other. The conversation was tense. Nearly heated. And for once, she knew she was at fault. Well, at least partially.

As her agent described why her latest book submission had been rejected by her publisher, Nikki glanced at her computer monitor, news stories streaming across the screen—an alert that yet another storm was rolling its way inland, the latest breaking news.

"What was wrong with the Bay Bridge Strangler idea?" Nikki asked, but deep down, she knew the answer.

Ina sighed audibly. "For one thing he's in San Francisco."

Nikki could imagine her agent rolling her expressive brown eyes over the tops of the bifocals that were always perched on the tip of her nose. She'd be sitting in her tiny office, cup of coffee nearby, a second, forgotten one, maybe from the day before, propped on a pile of papers that had been pushed to one corner of her massive desk.

"And you've never met him," she added in a raspy voice. "And since good old Bay Bridge is big news on the West Coast, I'll bet a dozen stories are already being written about him by authors in that enclave of mystery writers they've got out there. You know, I probably already have a submission somewhere here on my desk, if I'd take the time to dig a little deeper through my slush pile."

Another good point. Irritating, yes, but probably spot on. "Okay, okay, but I also sent you an idea about a story surrounding Father John in New Orleans."

"Who knows what happened to that freak? A killer dressed up as a priest. Gives me chills. Yeah, I know. He's a better match, closer geographically and infinitely more interesting than Bay Bridge, but really, do you have a connection with him? An inside look?" There was a pause, a muffled "Tell him I'll call him right back" on the other end of the line, then Ina was back, never missing a beat. "As near as I remember, Father John disappeared. Either moved on or, more likely, is lying dead in some Louisiana swamp. Crocodile bait or something. No one knows, and right now, not a lot of people care. He's old news."

"No one really knows what happened to Zodiac, and he hasn't killed in decades, but there're still books being written about him. Movies."

"Meh. From authors and producers without any new ideas. The reason your first two books did so well was because they were fresh, and you were close to the investigation."

"Too close," Nikki said, shuddering inwardly when she remembered her up-close-and-personal experience with the Grave Robber. That horrifying episode still invaded her sleep, bringing nightmares that caused her to wake screaming, her body in a cold, damp sweat.

"I'm not advocating you ever become a victim again, trust me. But you know you have to write something that you're emotionally connected to."

"So you keep saying," Nikki admitted as she looked around her little garret, with its built-in bookshelves, easy chair, and reading lamp. Cozy. Smelling of the spice candles she lit every morning. A perfect writing studio, as long as she had a story to put to paper.

"Here's the deal," Ina said. "The reason your first book worked so well, or at least in the publisher's eyes, is your connection to the story, your involvement. That's what you need."

"That might have been a once-in-a-lifetime thing," Nikki said as she twisted her pen between her fingers and rolled her desk chair back.

"Let's hope," Ina said. "Look, no one wants you to be a victim again. God, no. But you had a connection with the second book too."

Therein lay the problem. She'd sold *Coffin for Two,* her first book, a true-crime account of the killer she'd dubbed the Grave Robber, a psycho who had reigned terror on Savannah before targeting Nikki herself. She had no intention of coming that close to a psycho again—book deal or no book deal. *Coffin for Two,* into which she'd infused a little dark humor along with her own personal account of dealing with the madman, had sold thousands of copies and caught the eye of a producer for a cable network that was looking for particularly bizarre true-crime stories. The book was optioned, though not yet produced.

Her second book, *Myth in Blood,* also had a personal hook; she had been close to that true-crime story as it had unfolded. Working for the *Savannah Sentinel,* Nikki had pushed her way into the investigation, stepping on more than a few toes in the process and pissing off just about everyone in the crime department at the newspaper. That case, involving the rich and ill-fated Montgomery family, had had enough grotesque elements to appeal to the public, so another best-seller had been born. While trying to get close to that investigation, she'd met Detective Pierce Reed, and their relationship had developed to something deeper. Now they were engaged, and she was supposed to be writing book three of her publishing contract, but so far, no go. She just didn't have a story.

Ina said, "You know, dozens of true-crime books come out every month, but the reason yours stood out was because of your personal involvement. Take a tip from Ann Rule; she knows what she's doing. You've read *The Stranger Beside Me.* The reason that book is so damned chilling is because she knew Ted Bundy. She was there."

"She seems to have done well with other books, where she didn't know the killer."

"I'm just sayin' that we could use another *Coffin for Two* or *Myth in Blood.*"

"Or *The Stranger Beside Me.*"

"Yeah, I'd take that too." Nikki heard the smile in her agent's voice.

"I bet."

"You can come up with something. I know it."

"Easy for you to say." Stretching her back, Nikki stood. She'd been sitting for hours, working on a story for the paper, and now her spine gave off a few little pops. She needed to get out. To run. To start her blood pumping hard. For as much as she was arguing with Ina, Nikki knew her agent was right. She was itching to get to work on another project, couldn't wait to sink her teeth into a new book about some grisly, high-profile murder.

Cell phone pressed to her ear, she walked to the window, where she was lucky enough to have a view of Forsyth Park, with its gorgeous fountain and display of live oak trees. From her vantage point above the third floor, she could watch people in the park and look beyond the trees over the rooftops of Savannah. She loved the view. It was one of the selling features that had convinced her to buy this old, converted mansion with her advance from the book deal. She'd leased the two lower floors to renters and had kept the third, with this nicely designed loft office space, for herself. She was in debt to her eyeballs.

"Look, Nikki, it's getting to be crunch time. Maybe you should talk to Reed, see if he'll let you help with an investigation."

Glancing at the diamond sparkling on the ring finger of her left hand, she said, "Yeah, right. You know I won't use Reed."

"I know just the opposite."

Ina wasn't one to mince words.

"Thanks so much." Inwardly, Nikki winced as she glanced at a picture propped on her desk. In the photo, she and Reed were huddled close together, beach grass and dunes visible in the background, their faces ruddy from running on the sand. The wind was up, her red-blond hair blowing across Reed's face. They both were smiling, their eyes bright. The photo was taken on the day he'd proposed on that same beach.

So now she was considering compromising their relationship?

"Okay, maybe not *use* him, of course, but maybe he

could, you know, let you get involved in some way with a current case?"

"That's not Reed's style."

"Seems you managed to squeeze into an investigation or two before," her agent reminded her, and she squirmed a little in her chair. There was a time when she would have done just about anything for a story, but that was before she'd agreed to become Mrs. Pierce Reed.

"Forget it, Ina, okay? Look, even if I could get him to agree, and let me tell you that's a gigantic *if*, it's not like knife-wielding psychopaths run rampant through the streets of Savannah every day, you know."

"Every city, or area around a city, has bizarre crimes. You just have to turn over the right rock and poke around. It's amazing what you might find. People are sick, Nikki."

"And I should be the one to capitalize on that." Nikki didn't bother to keep the sarcasm from her voice.

"It's what you do best. So dig a little," Ina suggested. "Turn over those rocks. Squeeze Reed for some info on a new case, even an old one. There's got to be something. What are the police working on now?"

"Reed doesn't confide in me. Or anyone. It's just not his deal."

Ina wasn't persuaded. "Not even pillow talk? You know, men really open up in bed."

"Let's not even go there."

Ina sighed loudly. "Don't play the blushing virgin card. I know you, Nikki. If you want something, you go after it and, hell or high water be damned, you get it."

"Come on, Ina. Think about it. If there were another serial killer running loose in Savannah, don't you think I would know about it?"

She could almost hear the gears turning in her agent's mind. In her mid-forties and shrewd as hell, Ina was barely five feet tall and the only agent in New York who had wanted to take a chance on Nikki when she'd submitted her first manuscript. Ina had seen what others couldn't, and now, damn her, she was trying to wring out of Nikki that same essence and perspective for a brand-new *sales-worthy* story. "So get creative," she suggested, and Nikki heard bracelets jangling as she shifted her phone. "Maybe this time not a serial killer per se."

"Just a really sick monster with some kind of a blood fetish?"

"Or foot, or hand or breast. Or whatever twisted obsession turns him on." Ina gave a laugh that was deep and throaty from years of cigarettes. "Yeah, that would probably work." Clearing her throat, she added more earnestly, "You know the book is due in six months. It has to be published next year if we don't want to piss off the publisher and if we want to keep the Nikki Gillette brand out there."

Oh, Nikki knew all right. The date was circled in red on two calendars and highlighted in the virtual office on her computer as well. She wasn't about to forget, and she really couldn't. The struggling *Sentinel* was a slim remnant of its former self. Layoffs had been massive and painful. Nikki was working part-time for the paper and lucky to have a job. More and more, she relied on the advances and royalties from her books. Between the economy, the new technology, and her own ambition, she'd backed herself into a financial corner. She would be an idiot if she didn't make this work. "Okay, okay. I'll come up with something," Nikki heard herself say. As she hung up, she wondered what the hell that something would be.

She didn't take the time to think about it now. Instead, she flew down the circular stairs to her bedroom below, peeled off her jeans and sweater, and stepped into her running gear: old jogging pants and bra, a stained T-shirt, and favorite, tattered sweatshirt with a hood. She'd never been one for glamour when she was working out. Her running shoes were ready, near the back door, and after lacing them up and tossing the chain with her house key dangling from it over her head, she took off down the interior stairs and out the back, then sprinted around to the front of her home, ignoring the coming darkness. Her mind was a jumble, not just from the pressures of coming up with a blockbuster idea for a new book, but also from the fact that she was about to marry Reed. In her family, happily-ever-afters rarely occurred, and now she was planning to marry a cop—one with a tarnished reputation who'd left a string of broken hearts from San Francisco's Golden Gate to Tybee Island here on the Eastern Seaboard.

"You're a masochist," she muttered under her breath as she jogged in place, waiting for a light so she could run through Forsyth Park. *And deep inside a hopeless romantic.* The light changed, just as one last car, an Audi exceeding the speed limit, scooted through on the red, and Nikki took off again.

Starting to get into her rhythm, her heartbeat and footsteps working together, she ran beneath the canopy of live oaks, their graceful branches dripping with Spanish moss. Usually the park had a calming effect on her, brought her a sense of peace, but not today. She was jazzed and irritated; Ina's call had only added to her stress level.

Get over it. You can handle this. You know you can.

The air was heavy with the scent of rain. Deep, dusky clouds moved lazily overhead, and the temperature was warmer than usual for this part of November. She sent a worried glance toward the sky. If she were lucky and kept up her brisk pace, she might just be able to make it home before the storm broke and night completely descended.

With that thought, she increased her speed.

A few pedestrians were walking on the wide paths, and the street lamps were just beginning to illuminate. A woman pushing a stroller and a couple walking a pug made her feel a little calmer, because the truth was that Nikki wasn't as confident as she seemed, wasn't the pushy cub reporter who'd been irrepressible and fearless in her youth. She'd had more than her share of anxiety attacks since her up-close-and-personal meeting with the Grave Robber. To this day, small, tight spaces, especially in the dark, totally freaked her out. So she ran. In the heat. In the rain. In the dark. Even in the snow during the rare times it fell in this part of the country. She didn't need a shrink to tell her she was trying to run from her own demons or that her claustrophobia was because of her past. She was well aware that she was walking on the razor's edge of some kind of minor madness.

Hence, she flew down the cement sidewalks and cobble-stone streets, along asphalt county roads or muddy paths, speeding along the beach or cutting through woodlands. Mile after mile passed beneath her feet, and as they did, the nightmares that came with restless sleep and the fears of closed-in spaces seemed to shrivel away and recede, if only for a little while. Exercise seemed safer than a psychiatrist's couch or a hypnotist's chair or even confiding in the man she loved.

You're a basket case. You know that, don't you?

"Oh, shut up," she said aloud.

By the time the first raindrops fell, she'd logged three laps around the perimeter of the park and was beginning to breathe a little harder. Her blood was definitely pumping, and she slowed to a fast walk to alleviate a calf cramp that threatened, veering into the interior of the park again, only to stop at the tiered fountain. Sweat was running down her back, and she felt the heat in her face, the drizzles of perspiration in her hair. Leaning over, hands on her knees, she took several deep breaths, clearing her head and her lungs.

Straightening, she found herself alone. Gone were the dog walkers and stroller pushers and other joggers.

No surprise, considering the weather.

And yet . . .

She squinted and found she was mistaken.

On the far side of the fountain, beneath a large live oak, stood a solitary dark figure.

In the coming rain, she and the man in black were alone in a shadowy park.

Her heart clutched, and a sense of panic bloomed for a second as the stranger, an Ichabod Crane figure, stared at her from beneath the wide brim of his black hat, his eyes hidden.

Every muscle in her body tensed. Adrenaline fired her blood.

It was so dark now that even the streetlights cast an eerie hue.

It's nothing, she told herself, cutting her rest period short. With one final glance at the man over her shoulder, she took off again, feet splashing through new puddles, her lungs burning as she cut through parked cars, ignored traffic lights, and sprinted home.

He's just a guy in the park, Nikki. Sure, he's alone. Big deal. So are you.

Nonetheless, she raced as if her life depended upon it, and as the rain began in earnest, fat drops falling hard enough to splash and run on the pavement, she came around the huge, old mansion she now owned and, taking the key from the chain on her neck, unlocked the back door, then ran up the stairs two at a time.

Once inside her own space, she threw the dead bolt and leaned against the door, gasping for breath, trying to force the frantic images of confinement and darkness from her brain.

You're okay. You're okay. You are o—

Something brushed her leg.

She jumped, letting out a short scream before recognizing her cat, who was attempting to mosey through a series of figure eights around her legs. "For the love of God, Jennings, you scared the crap out of me!" She slid onto the floor.

When had she become such a wimp?

But she knew . . . trapped in the coffin, listening to dirt being tossed over her, feeling the horror of a dead body beneath her, the smell of rotting flesh surrounding her . . . in that moment her confidence and take-the-world-by-the-throat attitude had crumbled into dust.

She'd been fighting hard to reclaim it ever since.

She was safe now, she told herself, as she reached up and checked the door to see that it was locked a second time, then a third, and after pushing herself to her feet, she made a perimeter check of the house. All windows and doors were locked tight, and no boogeyman hurled himself at her when she opened closets and checked inside.

Unconcerned about Nikki's paranoia, Jennings hopped onto the counter while Nikki, still edgy, downed a glass of water at the kitchen sink and stared through her window to her private garden three stories below. Rinsing her glass, she sneaked a glance at the gate. Still latched. Good. She took another look around the garden area, with its small table and chairs and huge magnolia tree, now devoid of leaves, but saw no malicious figure slinking through the shadows, nor, when she stepped out onto the small balcony, was anyone hiding on the fire escape that zigzagged its way to the ground. Double-checking that dead bolt as well, she decided her home was secure.

Finally, she let out the breath she hadn't realized she'd been holding.

For the love of God, pull yourself together, Nikki. Do it, now!

Kicking off her wet shoes, she walked through her bedroom, where she saw her wedding dress, wrapped in its plastic bag, hanging from a hook on the closet door. Her heart tightened a bit, and she ignored the thought that perhaps she was marrying Reed for security's sake.

That wasn't true, she knew, peeling off her soaked sweatshirt and stripping out of the rest of her clothes. She loved Reed. Wildly. Madly. And yet . . .

"Oh, get over yourself." In the shower she relaxed a bit, and once the hot spray had cleaned her body and cleared her mind, she felt better. There was no dark, sinister madman after her any longer. She loved Reed, and they were going to get married. Her bank account was low, but she could sustain herself for a few more months . . . so all she had to do was come up with a dynamite story for her publisher.

"Piece of cake," she said as she twisted off the taps and wrapped her hair in a towel. "Piece of damned cake."

Within twenty minutes she was back at her desk, a power bar half eaten, a diet Coke at her side, her hair air-drying in wild ringlets. Scanning the newsfeed on her computer, she noticed a breaking-news report running beneath the screen:

Blondell O'Henry to be released from prison.

She stared at the words in disbelief. "No!" Quickly, she Googled for more information.

Blondell Rochette O'Henry, a beautiful enigma of a woman, had already spent years behind bars, charged with and convicted of the heinous crime of killing her own daughter, Amity, and wounding her two other children in a vicious, unthinkable attack.

Nikki's heart pounded as she remembered all too clearly the blood-chilling crime. Her mouth turned to dust, because Amity O'Henry had been her best friend back then, and Nikki knew, deep in her heart, that in her own way, she too was responsible for the girl's untimely and horrifying death.

"Oh, Jesus," she whispered, wondering if the report was true as she worked the keys on her computer, searching for verification of the story. In her mind's eye, she saw the image of Amity, who at sixteen was whip-smart and as beautiful as her mother, with thick, auburn hair framing a perfect, heart-shaped face, wide, intelligent eyes, lips that were sexy and innocent at the same time, and legs that wouldn't quit. And Amity O'Henry had the same naughty streak and sexual allure as her mother.

Nikki skimmed story after story, but they were all the same, nothing of substance, no details as to why Blondell was being released.

Nikki worried her lip with her teeth. She'd never really told the truth about the night Amity had been killed at the cabin in the woods—never admitted that Amity had asked her to come—and she'd buried that guilt deep. But maybe now she'd have her chance. Maybe now she could make right a very deeply felt and festering wrong.

Her search earned her an article about Blondell, written years before. The picture accompanying the article didn't do the most hated woman in Savannah justice, but even so, dressed in a prim navy-blue suit for her court date, her blouse buttoned to her throat, her makeup toned down to make her appear innocent, almost as if she were about to attend church in the 1960s, she was beautiful and still innately sensual. Her hair was pinned to the back of her head, and even though her lawyer was hoping she would appear demure, it was impossible to hide her innate sexuality.

Staring at the photo, Nikki knew one thing for certain: Finally, she had the idea for her next book.

As for a personal connection to the story?

She'd been Amity's friend. If that wasn't personal enough, she didn't know what was.

Chapter 2

Nikki drove like a madwoman to the new, downsized offices of the *Sentinel*. The newspaper had been a Savannah standard for generations, a bastion of the Southern press, but it was slowly dying, doorstep delivery and print pages giving way to electronic data zapped to computers and handheld devices, detailed stories cut into sound bites or Tweets.

Many of the writers she'd worked with had moved on or were contributing to the electronic blogs, posts, Tweets, and whatever was the latest technological blip in the ever-changing face of communications.

Located on the third floor of an old warehouse that had been converted to offices, the new headquarters were tucked into a weathered brick building that had stood on the banks of the Savannah River for centuries. Inside, the sleek interior, steeped in electronics, was about a third the size of the old offices where she'd spent so many years at a desk.

Nosing her Honda CR-V into a spot in the near-vacant parking lot, she grabbed her bag and braved the weather again. Dashing across the lot, through the rain, she skirted puddles as she locked her car remotely. A familiar beep told her all was secure as she reached the front doors beneath a wide awning. Into the building she ran and, with a quick wave to the security guard, took the stairs, water dripping from the edges of her coat as she used her personal code to open the door at the third floor.

With a click, the lock released and she hurried into the newsroom, where a few reporters were still at desks near the windows, separated by partitions, and the interior walls were dominated by a bank of computers for the digital feed. The employee lounge was cut into one corner, the restrooms another. Slick. Efficient. No unnecessary frills.

Few reporters were still at their desks, the day crew already having left and only a handful working the night shift.

"Hey!" she yelled to Bob Swan, the sports editor, as he appeared from the direction of the lunchroom with a folded newspaper under his arm. "Is Metzger still here?"

"Home sick." Shaking his bald head, Bob added, "Picked up the bug from his mother at the retirement center where she lives. Whole place is shut down by the health department. Quarantined. But not before Metzger got hit." Bob chuckled as he turned into his cubicle, and Nikki followed to stand at the opening near his desk. "Hear he's sicker than a dog. Maybe now he'll finally lose some of that weight he's been complaining about." He dropped the paper he'd been carrying onto his desk.

"Too bad," she said, without much sympathy as Norm Metzger, the paper's crime reporter, had been a thorn in her side for as long as she had worked for the *Sentinel*. "I saw something about the lockdown at Sea View on the stream at home," she admitted. "And I caught something else."

Above the lenses of his half glasses, Bob's dark eyes glinted. "Let me guess. About Blondell O'Henry? Helluva thing, that. But with Metzger down with the stomach bug, looks like you're up." Then, realizing he'd overstepped his bounds of authority, he added, "But you'd better check with Fink."

"I will." Since the Grave Robber story, Tom Fink had grudgingly allowed her to report some of the local crime, albeit they were usually the stories that Norm Metzger didn't want. Nikki had never understood why Fink relied so heavily upon Metzger, apart from the fact that the heavyset reporter was more of a veteran with the paper. And maybe, just maybe, Fink was a bit of a misogynist, compliments of divorce settlements by his ex-wives. Whatever the reason, he'd never really given Nikki the chance to prove herself. Hence her high-handed refusal to take over the crime beat after the Grave Robber case had wrapped up.

She'd thought she'd move on to a bigger, more prestigious newspaper in the Midwest or Atlanta, maybe even New York, but then she'd fallen in love with Reed and eaten a bit of humble pie, mixed with crow, and decided to work part-time here in Savannah, the place she'd always thought of as home.

However, since Metzger was home sick, this was her chance at a story that could go nationwide, be picked up all across the country, and gain her legitimate access to Blondell O'Henry.

"I assume Levitt is on deck," she said, mentioning the newspaper's photographer.

"You know what they say about assuming anything," Swan said from his desk chair. "If this *is* yours, getting Levitt is on you. And you might have to fight Savoy for him." Inwardly, Nikki groaned. Effie Savoy was a recent hire, a woman whose blogs on the *Sentinel*'s Web site were gaining popularity, a pushy reporter who was always around and dead set on being Nikki's new best friend. She was a real pain in the rear.

"Again?"

"She's a go-getter," Swan said. "Kinda reminds me of someone else a few years back."

"Yeah, right." She wasn't about to argue the merits of one of the newspaper's reporters, but it seemed odd, in this era of downsizing that, out of the blue, Effie Savoy had been hired to write a blog about all things domestic, and more. Her articles—or musings or whatever you wanted to call them—were all over the place, as was Effie. Nikki was forever running into the newbie, but somehow Effie had connected with the younger crowd. The worst part of it was that she reminded Nikki of someone; she just couldn't remember who.

Now she said, "I just thought I'd check the news feed."

"You'd probably get more info from Reed," Swan advised, raising his thick eyebrows.

"Not likely." That was the problem with this place. Everyone assumed she had a quick link to more information because she was engaged to a detective, but as she'd already told Ina, Reed was decidedly close-lipped about all his cases or anything to do with the department. She couldn't count the times she'd tried to gain a little info from him. Only three days ago, at the breakfast table in his apartment, she'd asked what she'd thought was an innocent question about a current case, and he'd just kept right on reading his paper, taking a sip of his coffee, even a bite of his toast, before saying, "Talk to Abbey Marlow," without so much as making eye contact with her. "She's the department spokesperson."

"I know who she is," Nikki had grumbled, tossing down the rest of her orange juice and biting back her frustration. "I just want the—"

"Inside scoop."

"Nothing like that."

He'd actually folded his paper onto the table and cocked his head, as if sincerely interested. Brown eyes, light enough to show gold glints, assessed her. "Exactly like that."

"It's just that you're the lead detective on the Langton Pratt case."

"And you're fishing again."

"I just want an angle."

"Seems to me you've got plenty." His razor-thin lips had twisted into a bit of a smile, that same self-mocking grin she'd found so intriguing when she'd first met him.

Infuriating, that's what it was, she thought now, as she knew she'd get no further with him than any other reporter on the street. "Reed's on lockdown, too," she said and headed for the cubicle she shared with Trina Boudine, who worked with human-interest stories and was her best friend at the office.

The two desks inside the cubicle faced each other and were separated by a thin panel with a few shelves. Trina's was neat as a pin, the desk clean, even her trash can empty.

Nikki's area was more cluttered and, as she called it, "lived-in," even though she worked only part-time. Pictures of her and Reed were pushed into a corner, along with a framed photograph of her niece Ophelia, known as "Phee," who Nikki could barely believe had started kindergarten two months earlier.

Plopping down, she unbuttoned her raincoat and let it drape behind her on the back of the chair as she logged on to her desktop computer and checked her e-mail. Sure enough, there was a quick memo from Tom Fink asking her to handle the Blondell O'Henry case as Metzger wasn't available.

"Yes," she said under her breath, happy that her name would finally appear in a crime-story byline again. It still bugged the living hell out of her that she was the second go-to for the crime beat, even after nearly being killed by the Grave Robber. It just went to show that, as far as editor in chief Tom Fink and the owners of the newspaper were concerned, it was still a "good ol' boys" network. *Such a load of garbage,* she thought, but she intended, once again, to prove herself and get paid while researching her next blockbuster. Smiling to herself, she started perusing the feeds.

The trouble was, she thought, as she scanned the bits of news that came through, Bob Swan was right. No doubt Reed had a lot more information on Blondell's release. "Bother and blood," she muttered under her breath, repeating a phrase she'd often heard from her late father, Judge Ronald, "Big Daddy" or "Big Ron," Gillette. Known for his sometimes salty phrases of exasperation in the courtroom, he'd been held in high esteem by both prosecution and defense teams. Big Daddy had been a fair judge who put up with little nonsense in his courtroom.

So maybe there was a way to get information out of her fiancé, she thought, as she searched through the press releases. She was certainly going to try. All he could say was no, which he was pretty good at, but for now she was stuck with the wire services.

And then she saw it. The reason for Blondell's immediate release: the recanting of key prosecution testimony from none other than one of the victims himself. Niall O'Henry, Blondell's son, now a grown man, was changing his story and saying that he was mistaken when he pointed a finger at his mother in the courtroom and, with tears streaming from his eyes and his tiny chin wobbling, had sobbed and whispered, "Mommy had a gun." Across the screen of her memory, Nikki saw him as he'd been: a scared boy, blinking in surprise, as if he couldn't believe what he'd just said. Then as the courtroom grew silent, every ear straining, he'd forced himself to say more, his little lips moving awkwardly as he struggled with the horrid words. He'd looked at the prosecutor and caught the slight nod; closing his eyes, he'd added, "Mommy shot Amity."

"I can't believe it!" Sylvie Morrisette raged as she took a corner a little too fast and the police cruiser's tires chirped. They were heading back to the station, and she was doing a good ten miles over the limit on Victory Drive. "That bitch should be locked up for the rest of her life!" She slid a glance at Reed and eased up on the accelerator. "Even that would be too good for her. I say, fire up old Sparky again and let her fry."

"Nice," Reed commented as they sped along the tree-lined street. Giant palms rose in the median of the boulevard, and large antebellum homes and live oaks draped with Spanish moss graced the sides of the street. "Were you on the force when she was convicted?"

"Hell no! That was twenty years ago." She buzzed around a green pickup that was loaded with landscaping tools and lumbering slowly. "How old do you think I am? I was still in Texas, probably mooning over Bart or some damned thing," she said, mentioning her ex-husband, with whom she had a contentious relationship. "But I remember it—boy, oh, boy, do I." Her West Texas drawl was becoming more pronounced, just as it always did when she was agitated. "She's an abomination to women, that one. Beautiful. Smart. And deadly as a cottonmouth, I'm tellin' ya." Reluctantly Morrisette slowed for a light, but her fingers held the wheel in a death grip.

She was a little bit of a thing, tough as nails, not an ounce of fat on her, mother of two and always, it seemed, pissed off at the male population as a whole. With spiky platinum hair, little makeup, and a quick temper, she was a definite force to be reckoned with. She'd given up her eyebrow studs and toned down her bad language as her two kids had gotten older, but she was still, as Kathy Okano, the assistant district attorney, had said often enough, "a pistol" in her ever-present snakeskin boots and bad attitude.

"You have to remember the case," she said, sliding him another glance. "You're a Georgia boy."

"I was in San Francisco at the time."

"It was freakin' national! All over the news, for Christ sakes. What were you, hiding under a damned rock?"

He didn't honor the question with an answer. "So refresh my memory."

She stepped on the gas and made short work of a Volkswagen Beetle that wasn't as quick on the draw. Whipping around the smaller car, she said, "The long and the short of it is that Blondell took her three kids up to a cabin for the weekend or something. Two younger kids up in a loft, Amity, the teenager downstairs, I think. Blondell claimed that an intruder with a gun came in, a struggle ensued as she confronted him, and everyone, including Blondell, ended up wounded. Of course, there was no phone in the cabin, and it was twenty years ago, before everyone and their toddler had a cell, so she tried to get the kids to a hospital, almost wrecked the car, and the girl died on the way."

"And the others?"

"Not good." Sylvie had turned grim. "The son, Niall, wounded in the throat, I think, and the little girl . . . what was her name?" Her eyebrows drew together as she checked over her shoulder and switched lanes. "Bella, I think; no, no . . . Blythe!" Snapping a finger, she said, "That's right. There was all kind of mention of Blythe's bravery because she took a bullet in the spine, ended up in a wheelchair."

"Sounds a lot like the Diane Downs case in Oregon years ago."

"That's the hell of it. People think Blondell purposely copied Downs. Saw a way to get rid of her kids and used it. Who knows? Reach into the glove box and see if there's any more gum, will ya?" She slowed and cranked the wheel, guiding the car into the parking lot near the station house on Habersham, a brick edifice that had originally been built nearly a century and a half before, as Reed found the pack of Nicorette and handed it to her. With the agility of a twenty-year smoker, she retrieved a piece and tossed it into her mouth. "I hate this crap," she muttered, and he didn't know if she was talking about the gum or Blondell O'Henry's impending release from jail. Probably both.

Morrisette pulled into a narrow spot and slammed the cruiser into park. "Here's the hell of it. Blondell had just recently miscarried when she shot her own pregnant daughter. How about that? It all came out in her hospital exam."

Now that she brought it up, Reed remembered something about it.

"She never said who the father was," Morrisette went on. "Was it her ex, Calvin? That might've proved messy as he was already involved with wife number two, who also was probably pregnant about that time. He would have been a busy boy. Holy crap, there must've been something in the water that year. Blondell, her daughter, and Calvin's religious nut of a wife, June, all knocked up, well, at least until Blondell lost hers."

"You're saying Calvin was the father of his wife's baby and Blondell's, before she miscarried?"

"That's exactly what I'm saying."

"You're not suggesting he was with his own daughter too."

"*That* never came up, thank God. Even though Amity was his *adopted* daughter. But no, I don't think so. I'm sure they would've been able to tell from the blood work. But he could've fathered his own daughter with June, wife number *dos,* and maybe the baby Blondell lost. Stranger things have happened." Morrisette shot him a look. "Then again, Roland Camp could have been the father. He was Blondell's most recent boyfriend. He's another winner, let me tell you. Not that it matters, as the kid was never born." She glanced out the window as a couple of uniformed officers walked past her car and into the building. "Or there's a good chance that Blondell's baby's daddy was some other lucky stiff entirely. Enough men around this town stared at her with their damned tongues dragging to the ground. She was smokin' hot. But who knows? I'm not sure the guy who knocked her up ever found out he was a papa, and since the kid was never born, the point's moot. It only matters because Blondell said in her testimony that she was drinking and confused because she was depressed about losing the baby. But that could all be bull."

Reed glanced at the station house, a beautiful building built for a much earlier time. Yet even with recent renovations, the offices of the Savannah-Chatham Police Department were showing their years.

"We're gonna have riots in the streets, let me tell you. Blondell O'Henry is one of the city's most reviled criminals." She cut the engine and opened the driver's door. "Look up the case," she advised. "It's got more curves and twists than a nest of sidewinders with stomach cramps. Flint Beauregard, he was the lead detective."

"Deacon's father?"

"One and the same." She closed her door as Reed climbed out of the car, and together they walked toward the main door of the station. The rain had temporarily ceased and the clouds were beginning to shift to let in shafts of a few receding rays of sunlight, yet Reed felt no warmth. He'd never seen eye to eye with Deacon Beauregard, who had recently been hired as another ADA, a lawyer who was just a little too smooth for Reed's taste and a man who, it seemed, rode to a certain extent on the coattails of his deceased father, a decorated cop whose reputation was nearly legendary in the halls of the station.

"The whole case was circumstantial, as I remember," she said as they walked inside, her snakeskin boots ringing on the old floor as they headed to the stairs. "The critical testimony was from the boy. And now he's recanting. Ain't that just the cat's goddamned pajamas?"

Chapter 3

Nikki read through old testimony, especially Blondell
O'Henry's, about the night in question. As she did, she
saw in her mind's eye the scenario that had unfolded in the
old cabin. It was a small building, one Nikki had known
well, as it sat on the edge of property belonging to her uncle.
Blondell was contemplating the loss of her unborn child and
her recent divorce from her husband, Calvin, whom she
swore was abusive. That's why she'd taken her three children
to the cabin: to think things over and get her priorities
straight. Her relationship with Roland Camp had been un-
raveling, and she had been faced with a future as a single
mother.

Blondell maintained that her two younger children had
been asleep, tucked into the loft above the main living area;
her older daughter, Amity, was on the pull-out couch downstairs. Blondell had been out back on the screened-in porch,
wrapped in a sleeping bag on an old chaise longue, drinking
wine and watching the rain pour from the heavens to dimple
the dark waters of the lake and listening to it pound noisily
on the roof. She'd said it was nearly impossible for her to

hear much of anything else, but she didn't mind. Caught in her own troubles, she'd been lulled by the wind and rain and wine while her kids slept inside the tiny cabin—basically one large room with a loft and a small alcove for a kitchen, along with a closet-sized bath.

She'd intended to bed down for the night on an old recliner near the fire that she'd lit in the old rock fireplace but had taken a few minutes to herself.

And that had been her mistake.

Somehow she'd closed her eyes and nodded off to the steady rhythm of the rain. She didn't know how long she'd dozed, only remembered that she'd awoken sharply at the sound of a car backfiring in the distance and just before a dog began barking wildly. The rain was still steady, but not as strong. She had a sudden premonition that something was wrong. Very wrong. And then her daughter had started screaming about a snake, a copperhead in the cabin.

Tossing off the sleeping bag, Blondell rushed in and saw, in the half-light from the fire, a horror that made her blood run cold.

A stranger was inside!

The fire had died down to red embers, so the cabin was nearly dark, but she could see a man's silhouette as he stood over Amity. He had dark hair and a muscular build, but his face was masked.

As he spun, Blondell saw the pistol clenched in his hand, above which, on his wrist, was some kind of tattoo.

The rest was a blur, Blondell claimed. She'd screamed and they'd struggled. She'd hit her head and the world went black for an instant, the darkened rooms swimming in her vision. She thought she'd heard a dog barking again. For a fleeting second she felt hope that someone was near, but hope vanished as her vision cleared. Amity was screaming that she'd been bitten by a snake, and the stranger, in the shadows, was leveling his gun at the girl. Blondell had wrestled with him but hadn't been able to stop the horror as he'd fired point-blank at Amity.

Blondell swore she'd screamed and fought for the gun as Amity, lying on the couch, moaned in pain and footsteps erupted in the loft upstairs. Frantic, she'd launched herself at the stranger just as he turned to face her, his gun pointed straight at her heart. She'd flinched, still struggling for the gun, managing to grip the barrel and twist it upward, and then she heard Niall cry out.

"Mommy! No!"

"Get back!" she'd yelled, struggling to gain control of the gun, but the stranger was stronger and twisted the weapon, pulling the trigger.

Blam! Pain jolted down her arm, and she lost her grip, stumbling backward and falling to the floor.

Dazed, reeling in pain, she remembered the rest only in flashes: blast after blast echoing through the cabin; Niall running down the stairs, then jerking violently as first one bullet, then another, struck and his body tumbled down the remaining stairs. Little Blythe chasing after her brother, only to be hit as well, slipping through the railing to fall to the floor of the first floor with a last scream and heart-wrenching thud.

Blondell had cried, "No! No! No!" as Amity, unconscious, was bleeding out, blood pouring from the wound in her abdomen. Her son and youngest daughter mowed down by the monster as well.

Barely conscious, she heard the dog again. Closer, she'd thought, but the stranger, rather than finishing her off, had suddenly fled, running out the door and into the rain.

Blondell's story was a chilling account, but it was at odds with some of the police evidence. No gun had been found. Amity had died on the way to the hospital as the result of the gunshot wound, though she did have puncture wounds in her leg and venom from the copperhead in her bloodstream. The snake's bite would probably not have killed her, but the bullet that cut through her abdomen and hit an artery had.

Blondell's two other children had been rushed into emergency surgery. Blondell herself had been treated for a bullet wound to the right arm and a slight concussion as well as a contusion to the back of her head. She'd obviously fallen or been struck, and there were scratches on her arms, all of which could have been self-inflicted. Her fingernails had been clipped, their residue, presumably, still in the evidence file at the police station.

Hospital workers claimed her emotions were "all wrong" for someone who had been through the type of trauma she described, that her interest was more in her own injuries than those of her kids. She'd seemed stunned when told that Amity was dead, but hadn't shed a tear. Nor had any motherly concern been evident while her other children spent hours in the operating rooms. When advised that Amity had been pregnant, her fetus dying with her, Blondell hadn't uttered a word.

Had she been catatonic?

Had her injuries so confused her and stifled her emotions that her reactions were out of sync?

Or was she a cold-blooded murderess who'd been sent to prison because it was determined she'd staged the whole horrific scene?

Nikki didn't know.

Had there even been an intruder at the cabin?

That too was murky, but it was possible.

The flattened body of a copperhead had been found in the muddy driveway. Even that was odd, for in the middle of winter snakes were commonly in a state of reptile hibernation, sluggish and dull. And then there was the cigarette butt discovered near the porch. Blondell didn't smoke that brand; in fact, she rarely smoked at all.

Nikki wondered. DNA had just begun to be used at the time of the trials, but now . . . ?

She thought of Amity, and her heart twisted in guilt. Could she have saved her? Hadn't Amity begged her to come to the cabin that night?

If she had, would Amity be alive today?

"Please come," Amity had cajoled into the phone. "I need to talk to someone, and you're my best friend."

"I don't think I can get away."

"But it's really, really important," she'd insisted. "About . . . about my boyfriend. You have to find a way to come and please, please, please don't tell a soul. If you do we'll both be dead." She'd seemed about to divulge some great secret, then said, "I just can't tell you over the phone. . . . *She* might be listening." By "she," Nikki had believed, Amity had meant her mom. "Come to the cabin, okay? I'll meet you at the lake. After midnight. Around one, okay? She'll be asleep by then."

"The cabin?" Nikki had repeated. "What cabin?"

"The one by the lake."

"My grandmother's cabin?" Nikki had asked, feeling a little jab of guilt for once showing Amity the family's nearly forgotten cottage on the shores of the lake when they'd been horseback riding. "How does your mother—?"

"Nikki! Just come! Nothing else matters," Amity had interrupted. "I'm not kidding. Please! It's a matter of life or death."

Nikki hadn't believed that plea. Amity had always been overly dramatic. Nonetheless, she'd reluctantly promised to show, to find a way to get to the lake, but she'd never made it. She'd set her alarm and even sneaked to the top of the stairs, but had heard her parents arguing in the den, just off the end of the staircase, so she'd waited in her room and eventually fallen asleep, only to wake hours later with the wintry Savannah sun climbing high into the sky, mist rising above the surrounding fields from the recent rain. Though she hadn't known it then, Amity O'Henry was already dead.

It's a matter of life or death!

She hadn't been kidding. Nikki had felt awful. Confused. Angry. Trying to convince herself that Amity's death was *not* her fault.

The news had rocked the community as it had ripped a dark hole of guilt through Nikki's soul. Could she have saved her friend? Somehow prevented the horrid tragedy? Sometimes she felt as if she should have been the brave heroine who somehow averted Amity's murder; at other times she knew with a bone-chilling certainty that if she'd made her rendezvous with Amity, she too would be dead.

As for Amity's whispered warning, "Don't tell a soul," Nikki had taken that to heart, never once mentioning their conversation to anyone, not even her uncle, who became Blondell O'Henry's lawyer. Not even when she learned that Amity had been three months pregnant at the time of her death, knowing her pregnancy had probably been the big secret she'd planned to tell Nikki.

Lots of conflicting evidence had been brought to the trial, and most of the defense's case was called "smoke and mirrors" by the prosecution. The whole case had taken on a carnival atmosphere, possibly because of the media circus that had ensued.

The prosecution had insisted that Blondell, estranged from her ex-husband, Calvin O'Henry, was involved with Roland Camp, a shady individual at best, a man who had no interest in raising another man's children. Speculation had run high that Camp was breaking it off with Blondell because of her kids and that, after losing her unborn child, she'd snapped. In a fit of desperation she'd tried to kill her own daughters and son, then blamed it all on a mythical stranger.

Did that make sense? No. But nothing else did either, and Blondell's disconnect over her injured children hadn't played well with the jury. Still, if she were truly guilty, she'd taken great pains, gone to horrifying lengths, to rid herself of her children in order to what? Hang on to the boyfriend who had sworn on the stand that he'd moved on already?

It was a terrible story. Cruel. Insidiously evil. An echo of the Diane Downs case that had taken place in Oregon ten years earlier. A case that Nikki, like many others, believed Blondell had used as a blueprint for her own heinous act.

The defense stuck with the unknown intruder scenario, the proof of which was a single cigarette butt left at the scene and the squashed body of a copperhead in the driveway. These pieces of evidence, they claimed, meant that someone else had been on the property. As for the gun residue on Blondell's hands, it could be explained by the struggle for the stranger's weapon.

Their take was that Blondell's own injuries were evidence enough that she wasn't the killer. The man she'd wrestled with, whom she hadn't really seen, his face always in darkness, had been in his twenties or early thirties, around six feet tall, with thick, bushy hair. She'd also thought he had a tattoo on the inside of his right wrist, the markings of which were unclear in the darkness; but in one of the gun's blasts, Blondell had seen something that reminded her of a snake, or serpent, or the tail of some beast. Most of the inking was hidden by the long sleeves of his wet hoodie. She'd been allowed to search through book after book of photographs of known felons and to speak with police artists, but she'd identified no one on file, nor had she been clear enough in the details of the man's features—partially because they were hidden by a mask— for the artist to come up with a clear picture.

The defense had insisted that despite going through the motions, the detectives in charge of the case had targeted Blondell from the get-go and had never seriously searched for another suspect, the real killer.

The prosecution's case was circumstantial and rested on the tiny shoulders of Niall O'Henry, who, because he was

old enough to know what was going on, was put on the
stand. It was he who, at eight, had, in whispered horror, sent
his mother to prison for what was supposed to be the rest of
her life.

Now that could change.

According to the information Nikki had gathered, Niall
O'Henry, along with his lawyer, was going to make a public
statement, his own personal press conference, which was
bizarre, but what wasn't about the Blondell O'Henry case?

Nikki had put in a call to the attorney's office, left a mes-
sage, and was working on finding a phone number or address
for Niall O'Henry. "In time," she told herself and kept digging. Since she'd arrived at the newsroom, the information
had started streaming in, and yes, she'd broken down and
texted Reed, but he hadn't responded to her bold question:
"Any news on Blondell O'Henry case?"

No surprise there.

As for Blondell, it appeared she was keeping her silence.
No one had any idea yet what she thought about her son's
turnabout and recanting of his story. Nikki had already sent
an e-mail to the warden at Fairfield Women's Prison near
Statesboro, requesting an interview, though she didn't hold
out much hope that it would be granted. Over the term of her
incarceration, Blondell O'Henry had been moved from one
women's facility to another and, since her one escape years
before, had been kept under maximum security at Metro
State Prison in Atlanta until it had closed. Afterward she'd
landed in Fairfield, which was a little more than an hour's
drive from Savannah. No matter what, Nikki determined, as
she left the offices of the *Sentinel,* she was going to get a private interview with the state of Georgia's most notorious
femme fatale and murderess, if it killed her. And, oh, yeah,
she was going to get it *first*.

She was already out the door when her phone chirped,
the sound of her preset reminder. She checked the screen

after she settled behind the wheel. "Right," she said when she saw the quick text that told her Mikado was ready to be picked up from the groomer's.

Fortunately, Ruby's Ruff and Ready was on the way to City Hall, where Niall's lawyer, after he'd filed the necessary papers at the courthouse, planned to hold an impromptu press conference. She wondered, as she backed out of the lot and eased into traffic, how the police department was handling all the unusual events in a case that had been decided nearly twenty years earlier.

Traffic was snarled in the historic district, but she knew the back roads and side streets over by the parkway. She took side streets to an alley where Ruby Daltry had her little shop. Hurrying, Nikki made her way through a short gate and along a brick walkway to the back porch. Over the screen door, hung a hand-painted sign, RUBY'S RUFF AND READY, in script, with colored paw prints of various sizes surrounding the letters.

She rang the bell and stepped onto the porch, where several dog crates and beds had been placed. A large, tile sink dominated one corner, and unmoving paddle fans hung from the elevated ceiling.

"Comin'," a voice called from inside, and Ruby, a fiftysomething woman with fading red hair pinned into a knot on her head, appeared in one of the three, small, descending windows in the door, walking awkwardly before reaching forward to unlatch the door. A child of about three, her hair in pigtails, was wrapped around one of her grandmother's legs and seemed fastened there. "I was wonderin' if you'd show up," Ruby said, offering a gap-toothed smile.

"Sorry about yesterday," Nikki apologized, stepping into a large open room to be greeted by a chorus of barks and yips. Three or four dogs, tucked into crates, peered through the mesh of their doors, and within his carrier, Mikado, ecstatic at the sight of her, was turning in tight, little circles.

"I'm glad to see you too," she said to him, leaning down and wiggling her fingers through the mesh. "Hang on for a sec."

Mikado yipped excitedly as Nikki straightened.

"You're not the only one who left a pup here. I don't know what people are thinking. Must be the rain . . . or maybe all that business about Blondell O'Henry. You've heard about that, haven't you?" Ruby was always one for juicy gossip.

"Only that she might be released, that testimony is being recanted."

"Unthinkable what that woman did," Ruby said. "Those poor kids. One dead, the other two growing up knowing their mother tried to kill them." She sighed heavily. "I just can't imagine."

"Blondell has always claimed that she was innocent, that some intruder came into the cabin."

Ruby's eyes met Nikki's in an "oh sure" stare. "What else was she going to say? That she did it? I don't think so. Nope, she's guilty as sin, and if you ask me it was all because of a man. She was involved with that . . . oh, what was his name?" She let out her breath in a low whistle.

"Roland Camp," Nikki supplied.

"Right!" Snapping her fingers, Ruby added, "A nasty one, him. Good-looking, I suppose, but a real lowlife. Don't know what she saw in the likes of him when, in her day, she could have had any man in Georgia, let me tell you. I'm a little older than she is, but I'm telling you all my brothers had their damned tongues hanging out at the thought of Blondell. Sickening the way men acted around her. Boys, men, she dated them all."

"You knew her?" This was news. Good news, actually. Another source of information. Even if it was, at the worst, suspect and, at the best, laced with gossip.

"I knew *of* her. She went to the school across town, but

the boys, they knew all the hot girls in the area, and by that time, I was out of the house and set on marrying Seth. Blondell, she had her eyes set on someone to get her out of a crappy home life, I think, and I swear she was involved with some older guy who was rumored to be the baby-daddy of her first kid."

"Calvin O'Henry," Nikki said, distracted; she clipped Mikado's leash to his collar and held him back as he strained forward.

"Uh-uh. He wasn't the father of her first baby, as I understand it."

"Yes, you're right. Sorry. Amity was adopted," Nikki corrected herself. "Mikado, slow down!"

"Who knows who the real father was?" Ruby went on. "The truth is, I didn't really think much about Amity, you know, until she . . ." Ruby glanced down at the girl still wrapped around her big leg and decided to let that thought go, but Nikki made a mental note that Ruby and her brothers had known Blondell as a young girl. Before she'd married. Before she'd had children. Before she'd become involved with Roland Camp and the horrid tragedy had occurred. Background information.

Ruby said to her granddaughter, "Come on, Janie, give me a break here."

Janie was having none of it, her waifish face twisting as she wound up for what looked to be a colossal wail. "Noooo!"

In a hurry, Nikki asked, "How much do I owe you?"

"Seventeen fifty. I clipped his toenails too."

She fished in her wallet and came up with two fives and a ten. "Keep the change."

Ruby's broad face brightened. "Thank you." She tucked the bills into the pocket of jeans that were a couple of sizes too tight and peered over Nikki's shoulder to the exterior door. "I hope the others come. I close up at five. Got dinner to get on the table, y'know. Seth, he comes home from the garage and he's hungry as a bear. Growly as one too, if dinner ain't on the table. Y'know what I mean?"

Janie was winding up again. "Hungry!" she cried.

"In an hour," her grandmother admonished.

"I want a snack!"

"You eat now and I know what'll happen. You won't want any of your dinner."

"Hungrrrrry," the little one insisted, grabbing hold of Ruby's leg again, clutching her rather substantial thigh.

"Oh, for the love of Pete. Here!" Ruby opened a drawer and pulled out some kind of packaged fruit snacks that looked suspiciously like red jelly beans though the wrapper proclaimed the health benefits of zero fat and a high percentage of vitamin C "in each and every bite."

Snagging the packet, Janie finally released her grandmother's leg and skipped off, her tears miraculously disappearing, her pigtails bouncing as she took off through an archway, separated by a series of child gates, toward the living room, where a television was visible, the screen flickering with the bright colors of a cartoon show.

"I swear, that one has me wrapped around her little finger, and it's worse yet where her granddaddy is concerned. Man oh man, does she get her way around Seth." Ruby was shaking her head as the beams of headlights flashed, splashing against the back of the house. "Oh, good. Looks like Margaret is here to pick up Spike. I was wondering. She's not the most reliable tool in the shed, if you know what I mean."

Nikki didn't comment. Glancing at her watch, she knew she just had time to run Mikado home before driving to City Hall to hear firsthand why Niall O'Henry had decided to change a story he'd clung to for nearly twenty years.

Chapter 4

*U*nprecedented was the first word that came to Pierce Reed's mind as he stood, collar to the cold wind, watching the growing throng of people gathered around the steps of City Hall. *Grandstanding* was the second.

Standing behind a podium that was set up under one of the stone arches of the portico was David Blass, a senior partner in the firm of Blass, Petrovich, and Sterns. A tall man with broad shoulders and what appeared to be an expensive suit, he leaned into the microphone. "Let me be clear," he said in a voice that boomed into the crowd, where reporters with cameramen jockeyed for position. He held up one hand, as if for effect. "There will be no questions. Mr. O'Henry is here just to make a simple statement."

The less-robust man beside him had to be Niall O'Henry, son of Blondell. He appeared uneasy, as if uncomfortable in his own skin, and was a good three inches shorter than his attorney. While Blass's skin was tanned by hours on the golf course, Reed imagined, O'Henry was pale in comparison, a smaller, nervous man in a much cheaper suit. His features were sharp, his lips tight, his eyes staring across the milling crowd rather than into it. Had he looked healthier, Reed decided, Niall O'Henry, with his large eyes, aquiline nose, and high cheekbones, could have been a handsome man. As it was, he had the aura of a trapped animal, ready to bolt at any second.

"This is all such bullshit!" Morrisette muttered under her breath. "Such bullshit!" She was chewing her gum as if by pulverizing it she could wring out the very last drop of nicotine.

"Mr. O'Henry would like to change his testimony in the state's case against his mother. Though the conviction of Mrs. Blondell O'Henry was nearly two decades ago, Mr. O'Henry was only a child at the time and now feels compelled to tell the truth." Blass stepped aside, his shock of white hair catching in the wind as Niall stepped up to the microphone.

To Reed, this smelled of total crap.

And he wasn't any more convinced when Blass stepped to one side and Niall, pale and wan, took the microphone.

His voice was thin and reedy, perhaps because of the injury he'd endured as a young boy, as he read from a prepared statement that he'd placed on the podium in front of him.

"I, uh, I just want to say that my testimony in the trial of my mother was false. I was young, impressionable, and confused. The night of the tragedy, when my sister Amity was killed, is a blur in my mind, still nearly a total blackout, and I, as a boy, was coerced into giving a statement that would ultimately convict my mother. I apologize to the state of Georgia, to my mother, Blondell O'Henry, and to God. Thank you."

That was it.

Hands shot into the air, and reporters barked questions, even though they'd been specifically told not to. They were ignored by Blass and O'Henry and were left dissatisfied, as was Reed, though he hadn't expected any major revelation in the first place, no new piece of evidence. The public and the police wanted something more. As he glanced around the crowd, he saw his fiancée, who, with her photographer, had pushed her way as close to the podium as possible. He'd caught a text from her earlier and knew that he'd be in for it later, that she was going to push him hard on this one.

But with Nikki that was to be expected.

"I'll meet you back at the station," he said to Morrisette. They had walked the few blocks over to City Hall to avoid the traffic knots and parking issues the impromptu press conference had created.

"Okay. I've already requested all the old files on the case." Her eyes narrowed at the podium, now empty. "Looks like it's going to be a long night."

"The first of many."

"Hell's bells. Guess I'm going to have to play nice with my ex so he can ferry the kids around. It pisses me off."

What doesn't? Reed almost asked, then bit his tongue as he knew that comment would piss her off as well.

"I'll be there soon."

"Pick up dinner, would ya?" she asked, heading in the opposite direction. "Your turn. The Dollhouse is right on the way. Get me a fried shrimp po'boy, extra sauce. With fries. And a piece of pecan pie."

"You want—?"

"Don't even say it, okay? I know it's a heart attack ready to happen. So bring it on!"

"I was going to ask about something to drink," he said dryly.

"Oh. Make it a Dr Pepper." And she was off.

Nikki couldn't believe it. As she watched Niall O'Henry being ushered away by his lawyer, she tried to step forward, to ask one of a hundred questions that leaped to her mind. She was thwarted, of course. She and a dozen other reporters were contained by security as they yelled questions at the re-treating figures of Niall O'Henry and his lawyer.

Thwarted, she turned to Jim Levitt. "Tell me you got some good shots."

"Nope."

"What?"

"More like great shots. You know, Pulitzer material," he said sarcastically while glancing down at her as if she were a moron. He was a beanpole of a man with sandy hair and freckles who'd played basketball in college and whose reach allowed him to hoist a camera over a lot of heads; hence, he was able to get shots a shorter person couldn't.

"Okay, okay, sorry," she said, sensing how touchy he was about his work. Levitt, whose wife was pregnant with twins due around Christmas, was feeling the bite of the economic downturn as well as the newfound difficulties of his profession. These days everyone had a camera, or at least a phone, that could take decent photographs. Not only was he used less at the paper, but his studio business had fallen off sharply. No one wanted to pay for professional shots when they could have Uncle Henry with a timer on his phone do a fairly decent job.

Working with his digital camera, he showed her more than a dozen shots of Niall O'Henry, his lawyer, and the group of people gathered at City Hall. "Don't worry about the pictures, okay? Just write a piece worthy of them," he said.

"Pulitzer material. I promise."

"I'll see you back at the paper," he said as he headed off, and Nikki experienced that same uncomfortable feeling that she was being watched. She glanced around. No one was paying any attention to her, not with the focus on Niall O'Henry. Though night had definitely fallen, she was far from alone, the crowd still slowly dispersing, a few knots of people still huddled together.

And yet she couldn't shake the sensation that unseen eyes were observing her, scrutinizing her every move.

Don't be nuts, she warned herself, glancing over her shoulder, her gaze scraping the shadows. Nothing.

"Hey!" she heard as she scrounged in the bottom of her bag for her keys. Glancing up, she spied Reed walking along the sidewalk toward her. As always, her heart did a quick little galumph at the sight of him. Yep, she thought again, *hopeless* romantic.

His gaze found hers, and his lips twisted into that irreverent grin she found so damned endearing. A five-o'clock shadow was in evidence but couldn't hide his strong jawline. Warmth spread through her—happiness—and she felt the corners of her own mouth lift. How could it be that she'd missed him when she'd been with him less than twenty-four hours earlier?

Make that ridiculous, hopeless romantic.

She ducked around a couple who were deep in conversation as they shared a cigarette and met Reed under a street lamp. "Where were you? I looked."

"To the side." He hitched his head toward an area that was now cleared of people. "How about dinner?"

"How about some exclusive comments on the Blondell O'Henry case?"

"Down, tiger. You know where I stand on that."

"Yeah, yeah, but this is breaking news on a very old case."

"Keep pushing, Reporter Gillette," he said dryly, then took the crook of her arm and walked her farther from City Hall. "Seriously, I've got to stop at The Dollhouse and grab a sandwich for Morrisette. I thought we could catch a quick bite together. That is, if you promise not to be obnoxious and keep bugging me for information you know I can't give you."

She was hungry, and she knew there was no way she

would be granted an interview with Blondell O'Henry tonight. However, she planned to be at the prison the minute the doors opened tomorrow. She hadn't had an answer to her e-mail yet, but she knew other reporters were probably clamoring for access as well, so she wasn't going to wait for permission.

"There's a certain amount of bugging I feel compelled to do," she explained, and he groaned dramatically as they linked arms and walked the three blocks to the small restaurant, located in a historic Victorian-era home that had been remodeled and retrofitted with a commercial kitchen, elevator, and veranda used for outdoor dining. Painted a soft pink, trimmed in white, with bay windows and a long porch, the restaurant did appear to be a classic dollhouse, and the owners, Kenneth and Barbara Sutton, added to the theme by shortening their names.

The restaurant was fairly crowded, but they didn't have to wait too long for a table, where they ordered meals for themselves and takeout for Reed's partner.

"Metzger's sick, so I've got the Blondell O'Henry story," she said, adjusting her chair. She was seated across from Reed, their table tucked into a corner of what had once been the parlor.

"I already know you're not going to let up until I give you an inside police perspective."

He didn't sound overly perturbed, so she added, "And maybe get a look at the old case files."

"You're dreaming."

The waiter appeared and set two glasses of sweet tea on the table. As he left, she took a sip, feeling the cool liquid slide down her throat.

"Come on, Reed. You don't have to give me any information that's classified or whatever you want to call it, nothing that would compromise the case, but—"

"What case? Blondell's been tried and that's it. If she gets out of prison, no matter what she did, she's free. If she's innocent, she paid a high price. If she's guilty, the nearly twenty years she's already served will have to be enough for the state. Either way, there's not really a case against her. The department will argue, of course, but when it's all said and done, she may walk. Guilty or not."

"But the case will be reopened," she said. "If Blondell didn't do it, then someone else did. Remember her story of the intruder breaking in."

"An intruder she didn't recognize. Maybe it'll be reopened," he said dubiously. "I can't say. I wasn't there. But Flint Beauregard, the lead on the case, is dead, so there's no help there. All I can tell you, as a reporter, is that the department thinks they got their man, or woman, in this case."

The waiter showed up again, this time with their meals—a steaming platter of fried chicken with collard greens and black-eyed peas for Nikki, barbecued ribs, corn bread, and slaw for Reed.

"So when are you going to the prison to try to get that exclusive interview with Blondell?" he asked, raising a dark eyebrow just in case she might try to deny the obvious.

"Crack of dawn tomorrow."

"I figured."

"It's my job, and I need to do it."

"No argument from me. Have at it." He was already digging into his ribs. "You know I'm all for your career—supportive as hell, as a matter of fact. Just as long as you stay safe, don't put yourself into harm's way again, and don't push too hard when you try to get information out of me."

"That sounded like a lot of rules."

He heaved a long-suffering sigh. "Maybe we'll agree to disagree for now. And then later we could . . ."

"Talk about the case?" She fought a smile.

"That wasn't really where I was going."

"Are you coming over, then?"

"I wish. I think it's going to be a long night for me and an early morning for you. How about a rain check?"

"I can do that," she said, hiding a stab of disappointment. Though she wanted to find out more about Blondell O'Henry, she let it go. For now. Pushing Reed only put his back up—in fact, he became a brick wall—but if she was patient and didn't badger him, he'd open up a bit. The trouble was, patience wasn't her long suit. For now, though, she decided, biting into crispy, butter-flavored chicken, she'd put questioning Reed on the back burner and concentrate on the O'Henrys.

Not only was there Blondell to interview, but her children as well. What was the real reason Niall was intent on changing his testimony? What about his younger sister, Blythe, wheelchair-bound since the terrible attack? And what of Blondell's husband, Calvin, now remarried? She'd known the O'Henry family far more intimately than anyone, including Detective Pierce Reed, realized, and she knew she had to jump on the story. Quickly. Before anyone else did.

They ended the meal sharing a large slice of hummingbird cake. As light as it was, Nikki could take only two bites of the banana and pecan confection. "Take the rest to the station," she said when Reed too put down his fork. "I bet someone there will eat it."

"Trust me, it won't make it past Morrisette's desk."

He motioned for the check. Once it was paid, they walked together to her car. "Going back to the office?" he asked as she drove him to the station.

"Working from home, I think. I've got to write the O'Henry article for tomorrow and, in the morning, drive to the prison."

"She won't see you," he said as she slowed for a yellow light two blocks from the police station. "Her attorney won't allow it."

"We'll see." As the light changed, she turned onto Habersham and eased around Columbia Square, where water cascaded over the ledges of a central fountain and stately live oaks stood guard over the pathways.

Slowing, she edged her Honda to the side of the road to let him out.

He said, "Be careful."

"Of what? I'm not going to compromise your case, I swear." She held up three fingers and mouthed, "Scout's Honor."

"I just don't like the idea of you at the prison."

"I won't be in any danger." She saw the doubt in his eyes and loved him even more. He wouldn't tell her what to do, but he'd worry a bit. "This isn't a case like the Grave Robber, nor is Atropos at large any longer," she said, citing the most recent incidents in which a deranged serial killer had stalked the streets of Savannah. "This is a cold case where a woman was charged and convicted of killing her kids. Family members. No one else was hurt." She paused. "That is, unless you don't think Blondell O'Henry is guilty?"

"I haven't studied the case, but since she was tried and convicted, yeah, I think she did it." He leaned over and brushed a kiss against her cheek. "I'll see you tomorrow."

Before he could reach for the door handle, she took his face in both her hands and pressed her lips to his. A warmth fired her blood as his tongue touched hers and her bones immediately began to melt.

"You're causing trouble," he whispered into her open mouth.

"I know."

He lifted his head again and winked at her. "Hold that thought, would you? Tomorrow."

"Sure, Detective."

This time he escaped, opening the door and sliding outside. As he jogged into the old brick building housing the police department, she nosed her way into the flow of cars and headed home. Traffic was thin, and she easily drove past the wrought-iron fence of Colonial Park Cemetery. In the darkness, she caught only a glimpse of the headstones, but even so her skin crawled, reminding her of her ordeal a few years earlier. Glancing into her rearview mirror, where the reflected headlights nearly blinded her, she made her way toward Forsyth Park and, across the street from its perimeter, the antebellum building she called home. The tiered fountain was illuminated, the tall trees with their canopy of branches ghostlike as Spanish moss swayed in the breeze.

"It's charming," she said aloud, "not scary." But she couldn't ignore the little drizzle of fear that slid down her spine as she parked, locked her car, and hurried up the interior staircase. On the third floor she was greeted by Mikado's sharp barks as she let herself into her apartment. The little dog spun circles and did a happy dance that always ended up near his food bowl, just in case she felt generous. "You're a little pig," she teased, picking him up and petting him, only to be rewarded with a tongue to her face and the not-so-pleasant odor of doggie breath. "First, outside with you, then I'll think about it."

Jennings had shown up as well and was pacing across the back of her couch. "Yeah, you too," she said to the yellow tabby before she found Mikado's leash and, as promised, walked him downstairs and into the backyard, where the porch light offered soft illumination and the patio furniture and shrubbery cast weird shadows. She stood on the old brick veranda, shifting from one foot to the other, a cool breeze cutting through her light jacket, her mind on the article that was forming in her mind.

All the while, as she waited for the little dog to sniff and take care of business, she thought of Niall O'Henry and how she would spin the story about him.

"Are you about done?" she asked and looked around for

the dog, who had disappeared into the shadows. "Come on, Mikado! I'm freezing."

No answer.

"Buddy?" Her gaze scoured the magnolia and crepe myrtle lining the brickwork, but she couldn't see the dog, nor did he respond. All she heard was the hum of traffic in the city. "Mikado?" Whistling, she walked toward the fence line, hoping he hadn't found a space to crawl under. "Come!" Her heart started to pound a little faster when she finally saw him, unmoving, staring toward a corner of the yard. "What is it?" He growled, and her nerves tightened, even though she knew he could be focused on a cat on the other side of the fence, or a squirrel or some other rodent.

Hearing the soft rustle of something moving through the undergrowth, the hairs on the back of her neck raised. Reed's warning, "Be careful," echoed through her mind. Shivering, she said, "Let's go, buddy," and quickly picked up the dog. His little body was tense, his ears cocked, his eyes trained on the encroaching darkness. "Give it up," she said, and scratched him behind the ears as she hurried into the house and up the stairs.

Once in her apartment, she snapped off the lights and moved into the kitchen to look down at the garden below. Nothing appeared to be out of the ordinary. When she squinted into the darkness beyond the fence, she thought she saw movement, someone hurrying through the shadows of the yard and alley behind her property, but she couldn't be certain and chalked the image up to her overactive imagination.

Mikado barked for a treat, and she broke a small doggie biscuit into two pieces before making a cup of hot tea. She then headed up the stairs to her writing alcove and computer.

The article came together easily, but there wasn't a lot of meat to it, nothing special, and she frowned at her cell phone as Niall O'Henry's lawyer hadn't deigned to return her call. "Par for the course," she grumbled and made the best of the information she had.

Tomorrow. If she could just get in to see Blondell, then she'd have a real story. Somehow, she had to make it happen. For now, she logged on to her e-mail account at the paper, found the pictures Jim Levitt had turned in and picked two. One was a close-up of Niall as he stood solemnly at the podium. The second was a broader shot that showed the crowd that had convened around the steps of City Hall. It still wasn't enough, so she searched through the paper's archives and located several pictures of Blondell O'Henry at the time of her trial. Even in grainy black and white, she'd been a striking, petite woman with dark hair that framed a heart-shaped face. Her features were even, her cheekbones sculpted. Her large, smoky-gray eyes were rimmed in thick lashes, and her full lips were parted, showing perfect teeth and creating a slight enigmatic smile that could only be called sexy. Despite having three children, she'd been thin, with a few curves that were, as her father had said often enough, "in all the right places."

After attaching the digital photos she'd chosen for the piece, she sent everything to the *Sentinel,* then started work on a synopsis of the book she planned to write. It would take her a week or two to put the idea together and then to flesh it out enough so that Ina and her editor, Remmie Franklin, would approve.

After working for two hours straight, she decided to call it a night, but as she was starting down the stairs, she spied her high school yearbooks piled on the bottom shelf of her bookcase. Her copies of the Robert E. Lee High School *Traveller*, named after the Southern general's famous horse, had collected dust since she'd moved in. Now Nikki walked up the stairs again and sorted through the four volumes to find the school year she was looking for—the last year of Amity O'Henry's life. Almost gingerly, she pulled the volume from its resting place to carry it downstairs.

Once she'd changed into an oversized nightshirt, she plumped up the pillows on her bed and settled in. Mikado curled up beside her, and Jennings found a spot near the footboard. Carefully, she turned the pages, spying pictures of classmates as they'd been twenty years earlier, wearing eager, fresh faces, once-cool fashions, and hairstyles that were no longer in vogue. She found Amity O'Henry's junior-year picture, and Nikki's throat tightened as she studied it.

As beautiful as her mother, Amity looked into the camera. Her dark hair fell past her shoulders, her big eyes a cool blue and the smile that touched the corners of her lips sensual. Not yet seventeen, she appeared to be a grown woman with almost innocent eyes. There had been something about Amity that had caused heads to turn and boys to fantasize.

And one had done more than that, obviously.

Amity had dated a lot of boys, her relationships as volatile and short-lived as a firecracker on a rainy Fourth of July, sputtering out quickly.

So who had gotten her pregnant? Flipping through the pages of the yearbook, Nikki saw the faces of the boys who had openly dated Amity. Brad Holbrook, the baseball jock, and Steve Manning, a do-nothing stoner who was Hollywood handsome, were the two Nikki remembered, but that was because Amity tended to date older guys, in their twenties— "men," she'd called them, though the ones Nikki had met hardly seemed like adults. Nikki, a year and a half younger, had been given strict curfews, and boys who dared to take her out learned very quickly that Judge Ronald Gillette expected his daughter to be brought home and walked to the door. She remembered one particularly excruciating experience. Tate Wheeler had asked her out, and upon his arrival at the house, they'd both been summoned into her father's den.

"You will have her home by midnight," he'd said, eyeing Tate as if he might be a deadly rattler ready to strike.

Standing in front of the desk where the judge had been seated, both Tate and Nikki had squirmed. Leather-bound books filled several tall cases that flanked the windows, while family photos, law degrees, awards, and antique weapons vied for the remaining wall space. Half-glasses at rest on his nose, the judge had selected a cigar from his humidor but hadn't bothered to light it, just fingered the rolled tobacco, as he repeated, "Midnight."

"Yes. Of course, sir," Tate had responded, and Nikki had withered inside. Why did her father have to be so old-school?

"Good."

Tate, in an effort not to shrink before the man, had said, "Nice guns," and nodded toward a wall of pistols and rifles mounted above a mahogany credenza.

"Thank you. I've collected arms all my life, and they each have a unique history." Pointing with his cigar at a long-barreled pistol, he'd said, "I have it on authority that this pistol was used in the War of Northern Aggression. I believe it killed at least one Yankee soldier, though of course there could have been more." His smile was cold as ice, and the look he sent Tate was usually reserved for prosecutors and defense attorneys who irritated the hell out of him in the hallowed walls of his courtroom. Getting to his feet, he added, "You know, son, this pistol is worth a fortune, I suppose, but the most important thing about it is that it still works. I took it out just last week. Hit a target dead on from twenty paces. The way I see it, a collection of firearms isn't worth a damn if the guns don't work."

She'd shot her father a "don't do this" look, which, if he caught, he'd ignored. "You kids run along. Have a good time." His fleshy fingers moved in a quick "be off with you" motion as he sat in his creaky leather chair. "And remember:

midnight. Not one o'clock, not twelve-twenty, not even twelve-oh-one. Midnight."

That had been that. Any hoped-for relationship with Tate Wheeler had died a quick death in the judge's den.

She'd been home by ten-thirty, and Tate hadn't called again.

"You're trying to ruin my life," she'd charged the next time she and her father had been alone. She'd found him at the fence line, watching his small herd of horses; two mares grazing in the lush grass, a foal frolicking on spindly legs.

"What do you mean?" He hadn't taken his eyes off the field, where sunlight had played upon the mares' backs, giving their bay coats a reddish sheen.

"All that crap about the Civil War pistol and getting me home by midnight! No one does that anymore!"

"I do."

"Old-school, Dad. You just like embarrassing me. You get off on it."

He'd chuckled, which had only infuriated her all the more.

"What I'm doing, Nicole, is separating the wheat from the chaff. Any boy worth his salt will be back again and not be intimidated."

"Don't you know how scary you are?"

"Not if you get to know me."

"For the love of God, Dad, no one gets a chance! You frighten them all away." She'd let out a world-weary sigh and watched one of the mare tails twitch at a horsefly. "None of my friends' dads pull this kind of crap."

"Watch yourself, Firecracker," he'd warned, using the pet name he'd given her. Then, less sternly, he'd added, "Have you ever thought that your friends' dads don't care as much as I do?"

"They just don't enjoy mortifying their daughters."

"Is that what I do?" He'd actually grinned.

"Yes!"

"Good." He'd slid her a knowing glance. "And if you think what I put them through is bad, just be thankful they don't have to deal with your mother." His eyebrows had lifted over the tops of his glasses, "Now, there's a woman who can be scary!"

Nikki sighed. No, Amity O'Henry hadn't had a father who acted like a medieval king who was dead set on protecting his daughter's chastity. Amity had been allowed to do what she wanted, with whom she wanted, when she wanted. All that freedom that Nikki had so envied had been a curse, and she missed her father more than she could ever have imagined as a teenager. To think about the last time she'd seen him . . . She closed her eyes at the memory, a frigid wind cutting through her soul.

"Don't go there," she whispered, chastising herself. To push the image aside, she found Amity's picture again and remembered her friend's last anguished plea:

"Please come. I need to talk to someone and you're my best friend."

And Nikki, daughter of privilege and harsh curfews, had failed her.

Chapter 5

As Nikki had expected, she wasn't the only reporter waiting to interview Blondell O'Henry. Though she'd arrived at Fairfield Women's Prison before eight the next morning, two television news vans were already parked in the lot near the front gates. One reporter, Lynnetta Ricci, a tiny blonde from WKAM, stood in position for an exterior shot of the guarded entrance, her cameraman already filming. Another team, DeAnthony Jones and his cameraman were finding a spot for the obligatory exterior shot of the prison.

There were others arriving as well, reporters she didn't recognize, but all sharing the same eager fever she'd felt upon hearing about the potential of Blondell O'Henry's release.

The gates opened electronically at eight, and they were ushered inside to a waiting area where they each showed their identification and turned off their electronic devices before surrendering them, along with their valuables, to a grim-faced African-American woman seated at a desk behind thick glass. Her hair was white and close-cropped, her eyes dark with suspicion. Her ID tag read Officer M. Ulander, and she didn't so much as crack a smile as she received the items passed through the two-sided drawer. Asking for their signatures, she returned visitors' passes with dexterity, if not pleasure.

Nikki hoped to be the first person allowed inside, but she was disappointed. She was third, behind Lynnetta Ricci and a man she didn't recognize, who had introduced himself as Ryan Nettles, a twentysomething, eager stringer for a newspaper in Atlanta. DeAnthony Jones had to settle for fourth.

She fidgeted on the padded bench in the anteroom, all the while cognizant of the cameras that were filming this sterile room along with all the other corridors and common areas of the new prison. The gates were electronic, the guards stern, the air inside the prison filtered and yet stale-feeling.

Her claustrophobia was trying to raise its ugly head. She hated the idea of being locked away, be it in a closet, a prison cell, or a damned casket.

The reporters before her filed in and out, and finally she was led by a guard through a series of electronic gates that hummed and clanged, her footsteps echoing on concrete floors as she was guided to an office on the first floor.

"Wait here," the guard instructed, pointing to another small, windowless office, where a receptionist/secretary was hard at work on the keyboard of a computer. A heavyset woman with streaked hair meant to conceal her gray, she wore a telephone headset and glasses balanced on her pert little nose. A nameplate announced that she was Mrs. Martha Watkins, and several plaques that had been proudly hung on the walls led Nikki to believe Mrs. Watkins had been an excellent employee in the service of the state of Georgia for thirty-plus years.

"Warden Billings will be with you shortly," the woman

said, not missing a beat in her typing, though she did slide a quick glance as Nikki entered and the door closed behind her, clicking loudly, as if it too were locked.

Nikki fidgeted in her seat for almost ten minutes before the inner door opened. A tall, serious woman in a slim skirt and collared sweater introduced herself as Warden Jeanette Billings, then asked Nikki into the inner sanctum of her office. A large window allowed sunlight into the room, where a Thanksgiving cactus was starting to show orange buds, and Nikki breathed a sigh of relief.

The warden's desk took up most of the office, where shelves of books and framed black-and-white photographs lined the walls. A laptop computer was open on one side of the desk and a tablet on the other. As if to add some age to the room, an antique globe, circa 1920, was positioned on a stand in one corner.

"Please, have a seat," the warden offered, and Nikki dropped into one of the two visitors chairs. "I received your e-mail about an interview with Ms. O'Henry," she said before Nikki could ask about it. "I did write you back this morning to let you know that Mrs. O'Henry is seeing no visitors." Her features were sharp, her demeanor that of someone who was used to being in charge. "Obviously you, and the others, didn't receive it or chose to ignore it."

"I was on the road."

One of the warden's slim eyebrows arched as if she doubted Nikki's word.

Nikki hadn't driven for over an hour to end up empty-handed. "If you read my e-mail, then you know I'm not just here for a quick article or even a series of articles for the *Sentinel*. I'd like to write a book, tell Blondell's side of the story."

The warden's smile was tiredly patient. "Again, Ms. Gillette, you're not the first. Ms. O'Henry has been approached many times by different authors interested in her story."

"But that was before. Now it looks like she could be released, a free woman for the first time in nearly two decades. I'd think she'd want the world to know how she feels, what really happened that night." Nikki was on a roll now, but she could see the censure in Jeanette Billings's eyes.

"I'm sorry, Ms. Gillette. There's nothing more I can do. I've passed your request along, with all the others, and Ms. O'Henry, under her lawyer's advice, will decide if she would like to contact you." She started to rise, as if the short interview was over.

"But I really would like to speak with her," Nikki argued, not budging. "I was a good friend of her daughter's. Amity called me the night she was killed, and I feel like I'm connected to it all in a more personal way."

Little lines of disbelief puckered the warden's eyebrows. "As I said, Ms. Gillette, I'll relay the information. Now, if you'll excuse me, I have to get back to work."

"I've met Blondell O'Henry. Spent the night in her house. Amity stayed at mine. My uncle was her defense attorney."

"Was?" She picked up on the one word she apparently considered a weakness in Nikki's campaign.

"Yes. Alexander McBaine."

"But he is no longer representing her."

"My uncle was forced to retire due to health issues, but I'm sure Blondell—er, Ms. O'Henry—will remember him and me as well."

The warden walked around her desk. If Nikki had made the slightest inroad past the woman's steely resolve, she couldn't see it.

"Thank you," Billings finally said, just as the door opened and the guard who had escorted her into the office was ready to usher her out again.

Great.

Just flippin' great!

She walked back through the series of gates to find

DeAnthony Jones glancing up expectantly as the doors opened and she stepped through. By this time there were two more people waiting, and Nikki would bet her next advance that they were reporters as well. "Good luck," she said to DeAnthony as he rushed past and she stopped to collect her things through the drawer of the glassed-in desk.

Officer Ulander, seated behind the thick glass, didn't seem any happier now than she had been when Nikki had arrived. "Sign please," she said in a raspy voice before she slipped another form through the drawer. Five minutes later, Nikki was out of the prison, walking through the cool morning sunshine to her car.

One of the news vans had vacated the lot, but Nikki knew there would be more. Blondell O'Henry was going to be at the forefront of news, not only in Georgia but throughout the South and perhaps across the nation, and Nikki planned to be front and center on the story.

She switched on the engine, opened the sunroof, and pulled out of the parking space. Since Fairfield was a new facility, the long lane winding to the main highway was smooth, the pavement unbroken. She glanced in the rearview mirror and saw the prison receding through the back window. Though modern and backdropped by rolling hills, the concrete-and-steel fortress wouldn't be mistaken for anything other than what it was. Watchtowers rose from the corners of thick walls topped with coiled razor wire.

Nikki thought of being locked inside and wondered how Blondell had survived all the years behind bars. She'd made it out once, during her only escape, from the first prison where she'd been incarcerated. For nearly three weeks, the news had been filled with images of officers and dogs searching for one of Savannah's most notorious convicted killers—on the run.

Nikki remembered that time because it was the summer

after her senior year of high school. At the time, Nikki was more interested in her boyfriend, streaking her hair, wondering how she would deal with being so far apart from Jonathan after their inevitable and oh-so-tragic breakup, which would happen as she went off to college. But the state had been abuzz about Blondell's bold escape via a garbage truck.

"Can you imagine?" her mother had said at the table on the veranda where Nikki and her parents were eating breakfast. Fingering the diamond cross at her neck, Charlene Gillette had wrinkled her nose as if she, herself, were hidden in those bags of sweltering, rotting garbage.

Their conversation had taken place just after the Fourth of July, and the Georgia summer had arrived in full force, the heat sweltering. "It's amazing that she made it out alive," Charlene said, adding, "Then again, I've heard that cockroaches can survive a nuclear blast."

"She's a tough one, I think," her father observed, reading the paper, a cup of coffee near his ever-present glass of sweet tea on the glass-topped table. The sun had already heated the flagstones on the veranda, and bees were vying with hummingbirds, whose shiny green backs gleamed in the bright morning light.

"More like callous. And heinous! Dear Lord, what that woman did was unimaginable." She'd physically shuddered, then sent Nikki an "I told you Blondell O'Henry and her kind were filth" look.

Nikki had finished her orange juice and ignored the fritters soaking up syrup on her plate, excusing herself quickly to catch up on accounts of the escape in the solitude of her room. At eighteen, in the throes of teenaged angst and lost in her own problems, she'd been awakened to her interest in the news by Blondell's bold escape.

In the ensuing weeks, the police had sent out a plea for

help in finding her, asking the public's help in locating the notorious femme fatale and her newest lover—oh, God, what was his name? Nikki had thought she'd never forget it.

Nikki flipped down the visor and concentrated. Barry something? No. Not quite right. Larry. That was it. Lawrence Thompson. Now she remembered. It had been Thompson who had been spied in a trucker's cap, oversized sunglasses, and newly grown goatee at a gas station in West Texas that happened to have a surveillance camera and caught the tattoo on his right arm as he'd paid for gas, beer, and chips. The inky head of a chameleon had peeked out of his sleeve. The cashier had seen it and recognized the tattoo as belonging to Thompson.

Within hours, the police descended on a fleabag of a motel southwest of San Antonio, where the pickup Larry had "borrowed" from his sister had been parked, dusty and baking in the pock-marked back parking lot.

He and Blondell, it was presumed, had been on their way to Mexico.

Upon her capture, Blondell was returned to prison, and her accomplice stood trial. Thompson had been incarcerated as well for his part in her escape.

Damn! Nikki *needed* to speak to Blondell.

She tapped her fingers on the steering wheel as she drove, then found her cell phone in the pocket of her purse and clicked it on. Sure enough, she'd missed several calls and texts while she'd been at the prison. After giving the screen a cursory glance, she dropped her phone into her cup holder as she considered her options.

Surely she'd get a little more insight from Reed, though she knew it wasn't going to be easy. Aside from him, she also had another source at the police department, a contact she hadn't tapped since the Grave Robber case, her brother Andrew's best friend, who had leaked information before. But if she contacted Cliff Siebert and Reed found out, there would be serious hell to pay.

That said, there was, as Big Daddy had often intoned, "more than one way to go at this," she thought, as she tore around an RV that was ambling along the road, filling most of the lane and making it impossible for her to see anything ahead. She did have an ace up her sleeve, as Blondell's attorney had been her very own uncle and, as she saw it, another personal connection to the story.

"Put that in your pipe and smoke it, Ina," she said aloud as she retrieved her sunglasses from a hidden compartment in the dash, then slipped the shades onto the bridge of her nose. Her mood elevated a little as she considered her next course of action after the bust at the prison. Of course, she wasn't going to give up on getting an interview with Blondell. Somehow she would manage to talk to the woman. She had to. Speaking directly to Blondell O'Henry would be pivotal for her book and would certainly add reader interest to the series of articles she hoped to write for the *Sentinel*. If she could just talk to Amity's mother, Nikki felt she could convince Blondell to tell her side of the story. Maybe Blondell would want money, but that could probably be arranged. Or maybe she just would finally want to set the record straight.

If she's not guilty, what if the police find another way, another piece of evidence to ensure that Blondell spends the rest of her life in prison? But no, she couldn't be retried for the same crime. That would constitute double jeopardy. Still, Blondell was far from home-free yet. The state of Georgia and the police department would want to see her kept behind bars.

It was time to pay a visit to Uncle Alex, Blondell O'Henry's onetime attorney and Nikki's favorite uncle.

Merging into the traffic on the interstate, she ignored the lush farmland and thickets of pine and oak as she drove toward the lowlands and Savannah.

The problem, of course, was that Alexander McBaine was suffering from dementia, most likely early-onset Alzheimer's, and so his recollections would be spotty and undependable at best. But surely he had notes from the trial . . . ? If she could just see both the prosecution's and the defense's sides of the trial—how perfect would that be?

"You're dreaming," she told herself, as she glanced over her shoulder, switching lanes to exit the freeway on the outskirts of the city. Still, nothing ventured, nothing gained. And just maybe it would be one of Uncle Alex's good days.

Chapter 6

"It's a mess, that's what it is," Morrisette said, eyeing all the boxes and chewing her nicotine gum as if her life depended on it. She and Reed had been summoned by Kathy Okano, who had asked that they meet in the training room that was to be converted for a special use: reconstructing the case against Blondell O'Henry.

The state of Georgia wasn't giving up on keeping one of its most infamous criminals right where she was.

"It's not just a mess," Okano announced as she joined them in the area that was being set up primarily for the review of Amity O'Henry's homicide. "It's *your* mess. I'm putting you in charge, Reed. And, Morrisette, you work with him."

"We have other cases," Morrisette said.

"Oh, I know." Okano, a tall woman with a blond bob, wire-rimmed glasses, and a sharp mind, frowned as she eyed box upon box of dusty documents and information that had been archived for nearly two decades and that were now spread over two tables. "And you can't ignore them, of course. But I'll spread the wealth, trust me. But for now, you need to lock this down. The press is already all over this case, and the department doesn't need any new black eyes.

"You two weren't here at the time of the trial, so you'll have fresh eyes. No prejudice. Unfortunately, some of the detectives who worked the case are long gone, and their expertise and knowledge would have helped. The DA at the time, Garland Brownell, died two years after prosecuting the case. Forty-nine and dropped dead of a massive heart attack after working out at the gym. Jasper Acencio moved to Phoenix five or six years ago. He's still there, as far as I know, working for the Phoenix Police Department, so contact him. Flint Beauregard, of course, was the lead. He died a couple of years back. Too bad, that," she said, shaking her head. Reed didn't say what flicked across his mind: the scuttlebutt that Flint Beauregard had died from complications of emphysema and congestive heart failure owing, at least in part, to too many years of cigarettes and rye whiskey.

"I don't know if Deacon can help," Okano went on, mentioning Flint's ADA son, "but maybe." Her gaze locked with Reed's. "God knows, he's chomping at the bit. Anything to ensure his father's reputation isn't tarnished."

Reed nodded. He also didn't say that in his estimation Deacon Beauregard was a class-A prick.

"DNA has come a long way in twenty years," the assistant district attorney continued. "If they can now prove that a handkerchief that was supposedly dipped in the spilled blood from Louis the XVI's beheading really is his, then we can certainly come up with DNA, if it's not corrupted, from that cigarette butt left at the scene, for starters. And find out about that damned snake. Why was a copperhead found flattened at the scene?

"Also, we've got a bit of a problem. Most of the evidence is here, but the tapes are missing. Videos of the crime scene and all the video from the trial, though I imagine if you dig deep enough you can find it on YouTube, or wherever. Everything else is out there these days." Okano glanced from Reed to Morrisette. "So if you see something that seems a little off, I want to know about it immediately."

Her cell phone rang, and she said, "Anything you need, just call," before clicking the phone on and opening the door to the hallway. Noise of the department filtered in: ringing phones, shuffling feet, buzzing conversation punctuated often by the ripple of laughter. Then the door shut behind her, blocking everything but the steady hum of the furnace.

"Jesus!" Morrisette shoved her fingers through her spiked blond hair as she opened an evidence box and peered inside. "What won't we need?"

"Good question." Reed eyed the crates, walking from one to the next. Everything—from the physical evidence, to the medical examiner's reports to the testimony at the trial—was there. Pictures of the victims and the crime scene, ballistics reports, hospital information, theories and interviews that had been bundled and locked away had been retrieved.

"Hey, here's something!" Morrisette said and reached into one of the boxes.

"What?"

She pulled out an evidence bag that held the well-preserved carcass of a freeze-dried snake. "What do you think?" she asked, holding up one booted foot. "If we crack this case and prove that good old Blondell really did off her kids, maybe I could end up with this bad boy as a souvenir. Get myself a new set of boots?"

"Yeah, that's what's gonna happen," Reed said as he pulled up a chair and scanned the list of evidence. It looked like it would be a long morning.

"You know your uncle is ill," Aunty-Pen said gently. The epitome of a genteel Southern woman, with polite manners, effusive charm, a dulcet-toned voice, and a backbone of steel, she added, "I don't see how he can possibly help you."

She led Nikki through the marble-tiled foyer and past a grand staircase that wound to the second-story gallery, with its coved ceiling and enormous chandelier, the one Nikki's mother had once referred to as gauche. The house had been built before the turn of the last century and remodeled at several points over its lifetime, so that it resembled a Southern mansion on the outside but was modern and efficient on the inside.

Ever the hostess, Penelope Hilton (no dear, not one of *those* Hiltons) poured them each a glass of sweet tea and offered Nikki a chair on the screened back porch with its view of her sweeping gardens of magnolia, jasmine, crepe myrtle, and gardenias. Paths wandered through the lush, fragrant foliage to fountains and birdbaths. She and Nikki had never been close, but that was just how Penelope handled all people—at arm's length. Though sisters-in-law, Charlene, Nikki's mother, and Aunty-Pen had never really gotten along. Their rift had widened considerably when Penelope lost both of her children in a tragic accident years earlier.

"Even if Alexander were well enough to help you," Aunty-Pen was saying, "he couldn't, you know. Client-lawyer privilege." She sat in one of the cushioned chairs near a round wrought-iron table where a vase of fresh flowers had been placed. Tall and athletic, Aunty-Pen had once ridden dressage for her college team, and as she'd been known to point out, had *almost* been selected for the Olympic team a quarter of a century earlier. Her hair was clipped short, a warm blond touched with gray, her eyes as blue as a Georgia summer sky. "And he's not here. I had to move him three, no, dear Lord, it's been nearly five months ago, though, of course, I do bring him home once in a while."

"I know," Nikki agreed. "But it would be good to see him anyway. The case is really just an excuse."

"You don't need one, dear," Aunty-Pen said with her cool, knowing smile. "He'd love a visit, though it may be that he won't remember you." A dark cloud passed behind her eyes. "His is a very insidious disease. Robbing the man of being who he once was." She sighed and sipped from her tea. "I'm going out to Pleasant Acres today, of course, and you're welcome to join me. I always plan my stays between his lunch and nap."

"Every day?"

"Mostly. Well, except Sunday, when I go directly after church and eat with him."

"I would like to see him."

"All this business with that O'Henry woman," she said, waving off the idea as if it were a bothersome insect. "I don't know what the fascination is, but then what counts for news these days . . . If it were up to me, they'd keep that woman locked up and throw away the key. My God, what she did." Aunty-Pen glanced out the window to a plaque she'd had installed in her garden, a stone etched with her children's names. "Burning at the stake would be too good for her."

"Innocent until proven guilty."

"Which she was. Proven guilty. That's why she's in Fairfield."

"But the prime witness recanted."

"Her *son*. A boy who now questions what he saw with his own two eyes. To think what he and his sister have lived through. It's impossible to imagine."

"Uncle Alex might be able to help me."

"I wouldn't count on it."

"Still, I need to visit him."

Her mouth twisted downward at the corners. "But you'd better brace yourself, Nicole. It won't be easy. You were, or, I mean, *are* his favorite niece, I know, but . . ." She shook her head sadly, then lifted her chin. Aunty-Pen wasn't one to wallow in grief. "We can go this afternoon."

"Good."

"Oh, and how's your mother?" She asked out of duty; they both knew it.

"Okay, I guess." Charlene Gillette, never a particularly healthy woman, had, in recent years, grown frail to the point that she hovered somewhere just above a hundred pounds, which wasn't much for even her petite frame.

"She's got to be ecstatic about the wedding, though. You're her great last hope."

"She's looking forward to it," Nikki agreed, but she bristled a bit, knowing what was coming next.

"You'd think Lily would settle down."

"She doesn't want to."

"But for Ophelia? What's Lily thinking, raising her without a husband?"

"It's the thing now, Aunty-Pen. Women don't need a husband to start a family."

"Don't be silly, Nicole. That's ridiculous! Any woman needs a husband, and certainly every child needs a father."

"That's antiquated thinking," Nikki said, and her aunt sent her a look guaranteed to cut through steel.

"You can be as modern as you want to be, but let me tell you, marriage is more than a ritual and a piece of paper. It's not just a privilege, it's a sacred union, not to be taken lightly. You're sure you're ready?"

"I think so," Nikki said, fighting her irritation. She knew the well of Aunty-Pen's grief and how it came out in these picky little ways. She would never get to be mother of the bride, never have grandchildren, or great-grandchildren. Rather than argue, Nikki changed the topic. "How about I drive this afternoon?"

"Let's just not speed as if we're running from a fire. The

world won't stop if we arrive at Pleasant Acres five minutes late."

Reed spent most of the morning sipping bad coffee and reading through Flint Beauregard's notes. The case file was thick and seemingly complete, at least at first glance, but he intended to study the notes in greater detail once they'd sorted through all the physical evidence, read the statements, and gone over the testimony at the trial. There were depositions to read, witnesses to find, and lab work to scrutinize and double-check with today's technology. Along with all the physical evidence found at the scene, there was a bundle of letters, yellowed with age, written in Blondell's distinctive loopy handwriting, all addressed to "My Love." None, it seemed, had ever been sent. They had been preserved in plastic, and as Reed read them, he felt as if he were invading a couple's privacy. The notes were intimate and sexy and flirty and spoke of undying love and desperate need, but gave no indication the author intended to do anything malicious or harmful. If anything, they seemed more like a plea for the same adoration the writer was offering.

Bothered, he set them aside and concentrated on the scientific evidence rather than the romantic yearnings of a woman who eventually would be found guilty of murder.

Meanwhile, Morrisette worked on organizing the evidence and sorting through what, in her opinion, was relevant and what wasn't. A junior detective was given the job of searching all the Internet databases looking for the addresses and phone numbers of the witnesses for the prosecution, as well as those who had spoken for the defense. The idea was to see if anyone else was changing his or her testimony and, if so, what would it be. The state hoped someone would come forward with more damaging evidence, but Reed wasn't betting on it.

Skimming the files, Reed made notes to himself. A few anomalies jumped out at him, not the least of which were Blondell's injuries. Had she somehow fallen against something on purpose to make it look as if she'd been attacked, and had she really fired a gun point-blank into her own arm to add credence to her story? If so, it was a gutsy move, but her injuries, for the most part, weren't life-threatening. No serious concussion or blood clot on her brain, no nicked artery in her arm. In that respect she had been much luckier than her children. While the defense had insisted she'd been wounded in a struggle with an assailant for the gun—hence the gunshot residue on her hands—the prosecution had argued that Blondell, a woman who could murder her own child in cold blood and try to kill the others, could certainly shoot herself. Reed wasn't convinced. Not completely. If she'd been dead set to get rid of her kids, why even drive them to the hospital? Why not finish the job and say she'd been knocked out in the attack, that the assailant had thought he'd killed her.

Why leave witnesses?

No, despite the outcome of her trial, it didn't quite jibe that she was a cold-blooded killer, so he figured it wasn't so much his job to find the evidence to keep Blondell O'Henry in jail as it was to uncover the truth.

Meanwhile, the press was all over the case, and he'd declined to take any calls he didn't recognize. The public information officer could handle any and all questions. Of course, that didn't include Nikki, who was already hounding him.

She was like a terrier with a bone when she wanted a story. He'd learned that lesson long ago, and while she'd irritated the hell out of him, she'd intrigued him as well, and he, who had sworn off women after the debacle in San Francisco, had found himself falling in love with her. He'd fought his attraction, of course, but in the end she'd gotten under his skin like no other woman, and he, once a confirmed bachelor, found himself proposing to her.

Now, as he looked at the autopsy report on Amity O'Henry, he inwardly cringed. She'd been so young, a child really, yet three months pregnant. He wondered if Blondell had known about the baby, though she'd sworn she'd had no idea that her daughter was even sexually active, let alone pregnant. Nor had Blondell been able to come up with the name of the child's father. Again, DNA testing would help, as long as the father was in the database.

Unfortunately, there was no blood, amniotic fluid, or anything from the fetus, and twenty years ago paternity testing wasn't as precise as it was today.

So who was the guy? Nikki said she knew Amity. Maybe she could provide a list of boyfriends the girl had been dating. Beauregard did have two names listed, but according to the reports, each had submitted to a blood test and had been ruled out as the father of the unborn child, whose blood had been O-negative, which, since Amity was A-positive, indicated the father had negative blood, a rudimentary identification test by today's standards, but still accurate.

His mind wandered for just a second to another paternity test a few years back, when he'd learned that a victim of the Grave Robber, a woman he'd been involved with, had been pregnant with his child.

His heart still twisted at that thought, and now that he was again dealing with a case in which an unborn child was a secondary victim, it made him all the more angry and determined to ferret out the truth.

Unfortunately, Beauregard's notes weren't as thorough as Reed would have liked, and the biggest piece of evidence against Blondell O'Henry—the testimony of her young son—was now being recanted. Reed would have loved to see portions of the trial, so he'd taken a quick look online and found some just-posted clips on YouTube, generated from the renewed interest in the case. He'd seen the defendant, demure and quiet, hands folded in front of her as the trial progressed.

Garland Brownell, a former football star, had handled the prosecution's case well, his style subtle when it was called for and more passionate when that was needed during the examination of his witnesses. Alexander McBaine had been as smooth as silk, a good ol' Georgia boy who oozed Southern charm. He too had dealt with each witness expertly. However, the cut-up pieces of the trial that Reed had found weren't cohesive. He longed for the missing tapes.

One thing he noticed: in every clip he saw Blondell was the same. Cool. Beautiful. Serious. Judging from her appearance, no one could have imagined her capable of the evil of which she was accused.

Now she'd served nearly twenty years of her life sentence in prison, which was nothing to dismiss, but there certainly wasn't enough other circumstantial evidence to back up that conviction, and, of course, she couldn't be tried twice for the same crime, should she be released. Was she guilty of the terrible, blood-chilling crime, or was she, as she had always maintained, truly innocent?

His job was to prove her guilt and allow the DA to pursue whatever path needed to be taken to see that Savannah's most notorious female criminal remained behind bars.

Surprisingly, his fiancée, Amity O'Henry's best friend, might hold the answers.

Rotating his head, he stretched the muscles in his neck. Nikki had been pushing him for information about the case. Now their roles were reversed, and he sensed she might be able to help him. If nothing else, he'd learn a lot more about the psychology of the victim.

Yes, he thought, kicking his chair away from the desk. The tables were about to be turned.

Chapter 7

Unfortunately, Aunty-Pen was right. Alexander McBaine wasn't the man Nikki remembered.

Nikki had driven the five miles out of town to the Pleasant Acres Assisted Living Center, a long, low building set on the marshy banks of a creek. From the windows of their units, the residents could watch waterfowl in the reeds, but the alligators were kept away from the rolling expanse of lawn by a sturdy wire fence that encircled the yard.

Inside the facility, she and Aunty-Pen had made their way along a carpeted hallway with handrails and evenly spaced pictures to a wing housing the patients with dementia, her uncle's new place of residence. Aunty-Pen had admitted that she did take him home on some weekends, just because it "broke her heart" to see him in the small apartment. She hoped being in his own surroundings would jog his memory, make him recall himself more clearly. So far that was a no-go.

Today, seated in a wheelchair in his studio apartment, Alexander McBaine was wearing a cardigan sweater over a white dress shirt that obviously had once fit and now was two sizes too large. Slacks that needed to be cleaned and slippers on the wrong feet completed his attire as he stared out a single window at a courtyard where feeders were attracting winter birds. Nikki's throat tightened as she thought of the strapping attorney he'd once been, a man who had commanded attention, whose sharp mind had been pitted against those of the prosecution. He'd had flair, brilliance, and a winning smile that had hovered somewhere between sexy and hard.

Now, though, his grin was that of a simpler man.

For a second, she thought he recognized her, but soon she realized she'd been sadly mistaken.

"Hollis!" he cried happily, and tears filled his eyes as he beamed up at her from his chair and pushed himself unsteadily to his feet. Standing next to her, Aunty-Pen stiffened and looked away. "But I thought . . . oh, thank God! Silly me! I must have had a nightmare. Yes, Pen?" He glanced at his wife, whom he obviously still recognized, then turned his attention to Nikki again. "I was afraid it was true, that you really had . . . died in an awful accident. But . . ." His voice drifted off with his confusion as reality and fantasy blended. Obviously, he'd thought Nikki was his long-dead daughter, her cousin Hollis, gone now, along with her brother, Elton. "Oh . . . dear . . . please . . . never mind. It's just good to see you." He blinked back tears, and Nikki, catching a look from her aunt, didn't have the heart to tell him he'd been mistaken, that she was really his niece and not his precious Hollis. Instead, she hugged him close. He smelled of the same cologne she remembered from her childhood, but now it was no longer tinged with cigarette smoke as he'd obviously been forced to give up the habit here at Pleasant Acres.

"How are you?" she asked, and he offered up a little smile.

"All right, I guess." He frowned a little then, his once-dark eyebrows knitting, his hazel eyes cloudy behind thick glasses that Aunty-Pen slid from his face.

"Look at these! How can you see anything?" she clucked, striding into the adjoining bathroom. Seconds later the sound of rushing water could be heard.

He chuckled. "Nothing's ever clean enough for your mother."

"She's my aunt," Nikki said. "I'm Nicole. Nikki. Ron and Charlene's daughter."

His expression went blank for a second, then worried lines etched across his brow. "Ronnie's girl?"

"Yes. Nikki," she repeated, smiling at him, and some of the clouds seemed to disappear for a second. "I'm a reporter with the *Sentinel*. The newspaper. You remember." *Please remember.* When he didn't respond, she added quickly, "I'm doing a story on Blondell O'Henry. You know. She was your client twenty years ago."

"Blondell," he repeated.

"Yes, she was accused of a horrible crime, of shooting her children."

He shook his head.

"She swore she didn't do it, and you represented her. She claimed a stranger burst into the cabin where they were staying and shot them all."

"All?" he repeated.

"Blondell was injured too. Shot at close range in the arm. Gunshot residue was found on her blouse and skin, and the prosecution claimed she did it to herself."

"Yes . . . Blondell." Was there just the hint of a caress in his voice as he said her name? Then his eyes clouded.

"You remember her?"

He nodded slowly. "Oh, of course I do. Beautiful woman. Interesting." His fingers moved a little, one hand straightening the cuff of his sweater with the other. "Not what she seemed."

"That's right," Nikki said eagerly.

"Dangerous. A siren . . ."

"Blondell was kind of a siren," she encouraged when he faded out.

His eyes focused somewhere in the middle distance, then he looked at her again. "Nikki!" he suddenly crowed. "About time you came to visit your favorite uncle!" Then he paused, his expression changing. "When did you get here?"

"Aunty-Pen just brought me." He was back. Even if he'd lost the thread of their conversation, she was pleased he knew her. "You're right. I should've come sooner. How've you been?"

He lifted a hand and tilted it back and forth. "I've been better, or so I've been told. Getting old is hell, you know. My mother told me that, but I didn't believe her." He nodded sagely. "Now I see she was right. It's good to see you."

"You too," she said with heartfelt enthusiasm. She hadn't realized until that moment how much she'd missed the uncle who had spent so many hours in debate with her father as they'd smoked cigars on the veranda, both of their wives disapproving, two women who had been forced into a reluctant, often competitive, and sometimes icy relationship by marrying half brothers.

But Nikki didn't have any time to consider family dynamics or loyalties, for she was certain her uncle's moments of lucidity were short-lived. "I'm writing a story on Blondell O'Henry," she said. "You remember her. She was your client, and she was convicted of murdering her daughter. She's about to be released from jail. Her son's recanting his testimony."

Her uncle's head snapped up. "No."

"No?"

"She's dangerous!" he insisted, nearly spitting as he grabbed her wrist in a death grip.

"But you tried so hard to see that she wasn't convicted."

"No. Nikki, no!"

"Why?" she asked desperately, hearing the water still running in the bathroom.

He glanced toward the door that Aunty-Pen had left ajar. "Leave this alone!"

"What do you know? Did Blondell really kill her kids? Uncle Alex?"

He was shaking his head. "Don't touch this! You don't know what you're getting into."

"Alexander?" Aunty-Pen called from the other room. "What's the name of your nurse? I want to talk to her." The water stopped running and Nikki held her breath, but then Aunty-Pen closed the door for some privacy.

Nikki seized the extra opportunity and said softly, "I want to know what happened."

"Attorney-client privilege, Nikki," he answered sternly.

"Can you tell me anything about the case? Something not privileged, but—"

"Yes!" he interrupted suddenly.

"Let me get my recorder and notepad," she said, throwing a quick glance at the bathroom door.

She heard the toilet flush as she dug around in her purse, just as Uncle Alex said firmly, "She didn't do it!"

"You know that for sure? How? Didn't you just tell me she was dangerous?"

"Did I?" He grew thoughtful. "I don't remember."

"How can you be so certain she was innocent?" Nikki asked. "Was it something in particular?"

He looked at her blankly.

"Of course, that was your position as defense counsel," she hurriedly tried again, "but you must've had your doubts or at least some proof to think that she was innocent."

She saw the clarity start to fade and wanted to moan with frustration. His strong jaw drooped, his gaze falling to the floor, where he saw a string and stooped to pick it up.

"Uncle Alex, how do you know that Blondell didn't shoot her children?" she asked one last time.

He plucked the string from the carpet and held it out

proudly as if he were a five-year-old boy searching for worms and had found a night crawler.

"I'm going to speak to the administration here," Aunty-Pen was saying as she returned to the room. "They're supposed to keep you and all your things pristine, and these," she held up his spectacles, "were far from it." Frowning, she set her husband's glasses onto his face, carefully making certain the bows fit over his ears. "Now, Alexander, isn't that better?" she asked.

He looked through the sparkling lenses and really smiled for the first time since his wife and niece had entered his room.

"Hollis!" he said, spying Nikki as if for the first time. Again tears threatened. "Baby girl!" His throat caught. "I thought you were . . . I mean, I dreamed this horrible nightmare that you were gone." He blinked back tears of relief and joy while Nikki withered inside.

"Oh, Alexander," Aunty-Pen whispered under her breath, turning away to hide her own emotions.

Embarrassed, Nikki said, "I'm not—" but stopped short when she caught another of her aunt's warning glances and quiet shake of her head. Instead she held her uncle's hands in her own and felt a cold desperation slide through her as she realized he had retreated again into the fog that was his mind.

Looking into his suddenly happy eyes, Nikki smiled at him and decided her aunt was right to not try to force him to recognize her. For a few seconds she could be Hollis. What would it hurt? He seemed so relieved to see his daughter that once again Nikki didn't try to dissuade him of a truth he so desperately wanted, even if it didn't exist.

A gentle rap on the open door caught her attention, and a young woman in bright scrubs stepped inside. "Oh, I'm sorry. I didn't realize Alex had company. It's time for his meds."